The Unfortunate Archibald Marble

The Unfortunate Archibald Marble

by
Elizabeth Waight

Illustrated by
Jenny Law

 Boll Weevil Press

Illustrations by Jenny Law

Book design by Dale Lyles

COMING SOON FOR YOUNG READERS FROM BOLL WEEVIL PRESS

Lichtenbergianism for Kids (a guide to creativity), Dale Lyles
Fish Sticks, Jeff & Natalie Bishop

For more titles, please visit bollweevilpress.com

This book is dedicated to you.
Be kind, be brave, and always, be you.

STANLEY
CRANKSHAW

SCARLETT CRANKSHAW

WILLARD
CRANKSHAW

CORNELIA
CRANKSHAW

LYLA
CABELL

ALEISTER
CABELL

ARCHIBALD
MARBLE.

Chapter One

Conversations In a Slightly Rusty Volvo

The sickly smell of peanut butter sandwiches oozed into Stanley's nostrils as his sister snored next to him. The sound was like a rusty trumpet.

'Are we lost?'

Mum peered back at him from the front seat of the car. 'No, cheeky, we're not lost. This map's just a bit... out of date.'

Dad dipped his head to wink at Stanley in the rear view mirror. 'What your mum really means is that *she's* been looking at a map of Cornwall, whereas *we're* in Yorkshire.'

Stanley laughed, flicking crumbs of cheese and onion crisps from the front of his t-shirt. 'Just use your phone,

Mum.'

'I've tried,' she snapped. 'There's no signal.'

'No way!' Stanley stared down at his own screen, horror struck.

'Ah, Yorkshire,' Dad went on, 'the most haunted county in England. Those wily whispering moors, where all breeds of spectral creatures lurk. Who knows, we may even sense the presence of a Barghest.'

'A *what?*' Stanley's eyes searched the sprawl of rocky hills surrounding the moving car.

'A demon dog, Stanley, that roams the countryside.' Dad stroked his greying beard. 'Some say the devil himself wanders here.'

'Don't tell him that.' Scarlett was awake. 'You know how scared our little Stanley-poo gets.' She smirked, poking him in the ribs. 'He's the only eleven-year-old who still sleeps with the light on.'

Stanley whipped around to face her. 'You can talk, Scarlett; you wouldn't even go in the kitchen yesterday, just because there was a spider in there.'

'Yeah, but it's *normal* to be scared of spiders.'

Stanley watched his sister's smug expression. At moments like these he was glad that, aside from both having Dad's jet-black hair and Mum's deep blue eyes, as twins they were hardly alike.

Mum's voice was shrill. 'There are no Barghests or devils where we're going.' She glared across at Dad. 'I wish you'd stop filling his head with such rubbish, Willard. I can't think of anywhere better to spend the summer. All that space and fresh air.'

'Cornelia, my queen,' replied Dad. 'I agree the house is a splendid discovery, but driving an overloaded vehicle through these crazy country lanes is no easy task. How about a bit of shush?'

Mum pushed her glasses up her nose and stared out of the car window. The cat eye frames against her white-streaked auburn hair made her look like a disgruntled tabby. Keeping quiet however, was not one of her greatest talents.

'It's just…' she began, seconds later, 'I'm really looking forward to this holiday. It'll be lovely spending so much time together as a family.'

Dad stretched out a hand to pat Mum's leg. 'I've no doubt it'll be a once-in-a-lifetime experience.'

'It's gotta be better than last summer's school camp,' Stanley agreed, shuddering at the memory. 'Remember that sweaty cook, Scarlett? The one whose nose dripped into the saucepans?'

'Urgh, I wish I didn't. I had to live on biscuits for a week. It was –'

Scarlett never finished her sentence. Instead, her mouth gaped so wide, Stanley could see chunks of peanut butter wedged in her back teeth.

The car had stopped at a pair of heavy iron gates set into a high brick wall. A name plaque was just visible through clumps of browning ivy.

'Marble Manor,' Dad grinned back at them. 'This is it, family.'

No one spoke as Dad hauled himself out of the car and made his way to what looked like a small birdhouse. A second later he was jangling a bunch of keys he'd found inside it.

'Exactly where they said they'd be,' he exclaimed, beaming.

The metal shrieked like a frightened pig when Dad dragged the gates open, their journey over the ground leaving deep rivers in the dirty gravel. Back in the car, he steered them along a winding driveway that divided a wild expanse of tree-lined gardens on either side.

Together they stared at the approaching house. Vast and ancient, its three storeys ended in a row of sloped attics, with narrow windows glinting in the afternoon light. Like watchful eyes, Stanley thought.

As the car came to a halt for a second time, Stanley stared at Marble Manor's crumbling walls; the finger-like vines clinging to faded red bricks were surely all that held these walls together.

A huge and ornate greenhouse completely covered the far left side of the house, splashes of fiery reds and yellows pressing against its enormous panes of glass.

'Er, how'd you find this place, Mum?' Stanley asked nervously. 'Doesn't look much like somewhere you'd go on holiday.'

'There, was an advert in your dad's archaeology magazine and we…' Mum's voice trailed away as she stared at the house, her face ghostly pale under pink blusher.

'I thought it was weird there was no website,' Scarlett piped up. 'No one would ever come if they saw photos of THAT.'

'Nonsense,' Dad exclaimed. 'A splendid Tudor pile, if ever I saw one. Although that greenhouse is Victorian, and those gargoyles look positively medieval.' He scratched his bushy head. 'It's probably a mixture of all three, with new sections added over the centuries. I could start an archaeological survey on all these layers of history.' The excitement in Dad's voice dissolved suddenly, 'If my job hadn't been cut, that is.'

Mum planted a kiss in his beard. 'It'll be okay, Will, I promise. You've got the whole summer to get started on that best-seller.' She smiled. 'And this place looks like it could inspire a few stories, eh.'

Stanley had never seen a house this big in real life and certainly never imagined one like it. It reminded him of a giant gingerbread house and his eyes wandered over the many protruding bays and turrets added to its vast flat front, like the sweets and candies stuck to the chocolatey walls in the fairy tale.

'Look at all those crows!' Scarlett shrieked now, pointing through the gap between Mum and Dad.

'Where?' Stanley's eyes travelled up to a sloping roof that seemed to bend under the weight of its many leaning chimneys and stone carvings of... what were they... *dragons?* And – how had he not noticed before? – the thick blanket of crows. Stanley's gaze followed one of those squawking birds as it took flight and disappeared into a dark forest of twisted trees that surrounded the gardens. A bee hum of fear murmured beneath his skin.

'That's odd,' said Dad. 'You never see crows in a flock like that.' He strained forward to better see out through the windscreen. '*A Rook on its own is a Crow, a Crow in a crowd is a Rook,* that's what my dear old Ma taught me.'

'But Maud never left London, did she,' Mum said now. 'Maybe birds act differently in the countryside.'

'Why would they?' The question knotted Dad's hairy

eyebrows. 'A crow still has a crow's nature, wherever it lives.'

Mum blew out her cheeks. 'Okay, so we've rented Count Dracula's weekend place. Good job there's plenty of outdoor stuff to do in Yorkshire.'

'That's right,' Dad said, his expression brightening. He gestured towards the hills and forest. 'We can go exploring.'

'Yeah, great,' Scarlett whispered from the side of her mouth. 'Weeks and weeks in the wilderness with no phone signal and no Internet, what's not to love?'

Stanley grimaced in agreement, but he couldn't help thinking that with a garden the size of four football pitches, its only fence made of huge climbable oak trees, a summer here might not be so bad.

So why did getting out of the car seem beyond his legs right now? He stared down at them, solid, but apparently filled with water, like they might dissolve into the seat beneath him at any moment.

'Come on, geek boy.' Scarlett dragged him from the car. 'Let's see how nuts this place really is.' She grinned, draping an arm across his shoulder. 'But if it's full of spiders, I'm sleeping in the car.'

Chapter Two
Marble Manor

The first thing Stanley noticed when he stepped up to the great front doors of Marble Manor was that their ancient wood was framed in silver and the floor sprinkled with a thick line of salt; salt that Dad's massive boot print had scattered in all directions. And this was only the start of things to come.

At the very centre of the house, the entrance hall was so wide and tall their entire flat in London could have fitted inside it. High windows looked down from a circular balcony, where Stanley could just make out thin strips of stained glass behind half-closed curtains. Gazing around the room in wonder, it occurred to him that the house wanted to keep its secrets hidden from the world.

The walls were panelled with wood the colour of conkers, a row of glass lamps casting a dancing orange glow over the objects hanging from them. There were masks and drums, maps and paintings; a three-headed fanged serpent with flaming red hair stared out at Stanley. The painting's eyes seemed to follow his footsteps as they echoed over the faded black and white floor tiles, his mouth slightly open as he took in the strange and spectacular sight of it all.

Halting in front of a cabinet filled with exotic stuffed birds, Stanley stared at their brightly coloured wings, stretched out as though in flight. Even though sorry that these poor creatures were long dead, he couldn't help marvelling at how perfect and beautiful they were, how the lamplight shimmered over their feathers, how alive they still seemed.

'It's like being in a museum, isn't it?' Dad grinned, gesturing at a row of high shelves that held animal skeletons, armour-plated insects, bowls of crystals, shells and acorns. 'More rarities than the Pitt-Rivers Museum in Oxford.' He grabbed a pair of silver bells, holding one in each hand and ringing them above his head. 'Cornelia!' he bellowed, before disappearing through a doorway in search of her.

In that same moment came a chorus of clock chimes. Stanley looked up to find that one wall was completely covered in them. In the very centre was a cuckoo clock. Rather than a cuckoo, this one had a hummingbird fluttering out from inside it. Something flipped in Stanley's stomach; for a moment he was sure the hummingbird's shimmering turquoise wings had been flying free, not attached to the clock at all.

'As if,' he muttered, turning instead towards the sound of Mum's voice calling his name.

All the doors on the right side of the hall were shut and padlocked, and there were so many opening off to the left it was impossible to tell which room Mum might be in. Stanley's eyes travelled up the wide staircase covered with thick red carpet, leading to landings on both sides and the many first-floor bedrooms. His gaze followed the carpet deeper into the house, a wish to see more travelling with it. But something stopped him, and he held onto that curiosity for now, pulling it back towards him like a sticky thread of spider's web.

'Stanley, are you out there?' Scarlett's voice had come from one of the open doors downstairs. He found her standing in a high-ceilinged dining room, grinning up at a statue of a bearded man in robes, his arm resting on a serpent-entwined staff.

'Who invited *him* for dinner?' she giggled, turning to face Stanley. He considered the statue for a moment; it looked familiar.

'Bit weird, don't you think?' Scarlett said.

'I'm not sure there'll be anything in this house that isn't w–' The word dropped from Stanley's lips. Through an open door in the dining room he could see a living room behind it, where right in the centre, as though it were the most natural place for it, sat a wooden canoe.

Stanley's frown melted into a smile. 'Ahoy there, shipmates!' he called, walking into the living room, hopping into the canoe and grabbing the oars. 'A storm's a brewin' and the seas are rough.'

A muffled snigger made him stop. He spun in his seat,

expecting to find Scarlett in the doorway. There was no one there. The hot breath of fear tingled his neck: there was no one else in the room at all.

'Hello...?' Stanley dropped the oars and leapt to his feet. A rustling sound was coming from across the room, but in such a large space it was hard to tell exactly where the sound had come from. His eyes were drawn to a long pink and gold sofa sitting close to the back wall. Yes, there was the sound again, like someone was crawling over newspapers.

Tiptoeing over the worn-out carpet, Stanley peered behind the sofa, only to find piles of old books and newspapers. Nothing else. Except – he stared at the wall behind the sofa, blinking at a small metal something that sparkled in the afternoon light. Moving closer he saw it was an iron door handle in the shape of a scorpion. He hadn't noticed this door before, probably due to the fact that its wood was faded and pale like the brown wallpaper around it.

Stanley's fingers felt the detailed metalwork of the scorpion's tail as he closed his hand around the handle and pulled. While the door had no keyhole, it was locked, and even when pushing and pulling until his fingers ached the door still wouldn't budge. Was it glued shut? He put his ear to the wood. Just like the handle the door was cold, and there were sighs of wind behind it, like a low voice whispering.

'Nelly!' Dad's voice boomed suddenly, making Stanley nearly jump out of his skin. He wasn't sure why he did it, but he jumped away from the door and onto the back of the sofa. He sat there now, lounging awkwardly and waiting for Dad to appear.

'Cornelia!' Dad bellowed again. Stanley could hear his

footsteps bounding around the hallway. 'Have you seen my wash bag? I've got something rather unpleasant in my ear.'

Dad walked into the living room, stopping in front of Stanley. 'And what are you doing up there, sunshine?' A mischievous smile danced inside Dad's beard. He plunged a finger into his ear, extracted a lump of wax, eyed it with pride, and then wiped it down the back of his trousers. Stanley watched the earwax peel itself free and plop to the floor. 'Didn't need my wash bag after all,' he said, winking at Stanley.

When Mum appeared, her mouth was so tight she looked like she'd swallowed her lips. 'It's not quite as they described, is it,' she said, waving her arms around the room. 'And they *promised* they'd store a lot of the old man's things in the east wing. It's only the west wing we've rented, after all.' She sighed, wiping dusty hands over the skirt on her ample bottom.

'Ha!' Dad yelled. 'I told you not to believe a word that pair told us. He wore a spotted bow-tie, for heaven's sake, and what about that moustache?' Dad spied the canoe and within seconds had seated himself inside, laughing as he reached for the oars. 'Anyone who waxes his facial hair into a shape like *that,* shouldn't be allowed into positions of trust, that's for certain.'

At this, Mum's mouth twitched into a smile. 'We'll just have to make the best of it, I suppose,' she said, walking out of the room. 'At least it was cheap.' She blushed, turning quickly back to face him. 'Oh, sorry, Will, I didn't mean… Shall we get our stuff in before it gets dark?'

'For you, my beloved, anything,' Dad smiled. 'Come on,

Stanley, you can help.'

When Stanley jumped down from the sofa, his breath caught in his throat. A fox lay curled up on an armchair, its bushy tail coiled and its small red face resting on outstretched paws. Creeping towards it, Stanley stopped for a moment, staring into the animal's eyes. They were half closed and unblinking. It was stuffed – of course it was. Yet, it was eerily real, almost as if the soft fur of its back was rising and falling gently. He knew he was being stupid, but what if...? Very slowly he edged a hand forwards until it almost reached the fox's face.

'Don't touch it!' Scarlett yelled from behind him. 'It's probably still got fleas.' She studied the creature curiously, her words carrying their usual sting, 'I've read about taxidermy. Why would anyone wanna keep dead animals in the house? Talk about manky.'

Stanley's arms dropped to his side. 'I know, gross,' he said, forcing a smile. He had to stop imagining these strange and unlikely things. 'Flights of fancy' his mum called them. 'Living in a dream world,' his teachers often complained; and while his friends just laughed it off, he'd heard the 'weirdo' rumours about him from the other kids at school.

Well not any more. This summer he would train his brain to shut this stuff out, just like the school counsellor had taught him. He would be like everyone else. Not weird. Not different. Just normal.

Still, following Scarlett to the front door, Stanley felt his breathing quicken. He knew the house was old, and most of its contents were too, judging by the state of them; but he'd been in plenty of places suffering from dust and damp – Uncle

Brian's boat in Bognor Regis being a prime example. No, there was something more than dust and damp in the air here, something that danced in his nostrils; something that was slowly beginning to make his skin prickle and his eyes water.

Chapter Three

The Eyes

Stanley was alone in the greenhouse. He found the warmth and light in here comforting after the murky strangeness of the main house. Tendrils of lush green vines crept over every surface, weaving around the iron window frames and eventually pressing against the glass of a high domed ceiling. Here and there sprung sweet smelling flowers in vivid electric colours and with stiff pointy leaves; many looking uncannily like the fantastical creatures in the entrance hall paintings.

Long benches were packed with plants and herbs, the air thick with the warm smell of damp soil. Many of the leaves and petals held perfect droplets of water, and when Stanley poked his fingers into the pots he felt the wetness of the earth on his hands. The plants had been watered, he realised with a start. In fact everything in the greenhouse was well-tended, loved even. It was all so different from the neglected feel of the main house.

A tapping sound made him look up. Mum was staring in from outside. 'What are you doing?' she mouthed though the glass, then came around and stuck her head through the doorway. 'Wow, this really is a hothouse!' She fanned the neck of her jumper, her bright eyes flitting around. 'Are we expected to water all these plants? No one mentioned anything to me about a gardener coming.' She turned to Stanley. 'Have you decided which bedroom you'd like?'

None of them if he were honest, Stanley thought. He shrugged and said, 'Maybe the small one at the back?' Yes, he'd feel calmer in a smaller room. You could see all four corners at once.

Mum screwed her face up. 'That one's pretty far from ours, won't you be a bit, well – you know…'

'Mum, I'm not a baby.' Heat throbbed in Stanley's cheeks. 'I won't be *scared*.'

Mum stepped inside. 'I know, I'm sorry.' She laid a hand on his arm and he smiled. 'At least I'll know if danger's coming,' he said. 'I saw a crystal ball in that room.'

Mum shook her head, laughing. 'The only danger you'll face in this house is the junk obstacle course.' She steered Stanley out of the greenhouse and towards the living room, where they soon found Dad and Scarlett arguing.

Stanley sniffed the air; the thick sweet smell of the greenhouse had followed them in.

'Why should I have to touch an old man's disgusting false teeth?' Scarlett demanded. She was clutching a glass of water with something green floating in it. 'Look!' She thrust the glass at Dad. 'They've got *algae* growing on them!'

Dad grabbed the glass, plucking the teeth out of the water. 'No we don't,' he said, in a dopey voice, snapping the teeth in front of Scarlett like they were talking. 'How dare you mock our posh green coat? No dress sense, these kids today.'

'Come on, Scarlett,' Mum said, trying not to laugh. '*I'll* help you clear your room out.'

Stanley felt his muscles relax. If Dad could have fun in this crazy old house, then surely he could too.

'Come back soon, dumplings,' Dad shouted after them, using the false teeth to talk again.

Stanley opened his mouth to laugh, but someone beat him to it. There was no mistaking it this time; that sniggering definitely hadn't come from a voice belonging to a Crankshaw; someone else *must* be in the house with them. An uneasy thought struck him. Was Marble Manor the place to go for dares? He could easily imagine the village kids all shoving each other to get a good look inside this creepy place. 'I bet that's what's going on,' he muttered, anger washing away the fear.

Marching around the room, Stanley threw open the rickety cabinets and pulled back thick, mildewed curtains. There was no one lurking among the cobwebs. Then, as he walked out into the hallway, another creepy question seeped into his mind: was he even sure that laughter had come from a kid? Icy fingers stroked his spine. If he thought about it, the voice had sounded more like an old lady's. Stanley whipped around; out of one eye he'd just seen something move.

'If you're okay on your own for a bit,' Dad called out, 'I'm off to see what else is lurking in that garden shed. I found some interesting recipes hidden inside an old Welly boot, earlier.' He laughed, mumbling to himself as he made his way across the hallway. 'They certainly beat your mum's beetroot and black pudding kebabs.

Stanley tried to reply but his voice was hiding somewhere behind his tonsils. He was desperate for Dad to stay, but the huge man had disappeared out of the front doors before Stanley could locate his voice and stop him.

Swallowing hard, Stanley turned his head to where he'd seen the movement, his eyes landing on a cupboard built into the left side of the long staircase. A cupboard whose door was half open. His heartbeat pulsating in his eardrums, he crept closer, just enough to see inside. It was as black as those crows on the roof. All he could see was a long saggy cobweb stretching from the open door to deep inside. Stanley fought to focus his eyes – there *had* to be someone hiding in there.

'What are you looking at?' Mum's voice had come from the long balcony above that looped the entrance hall.

Stanley glanced up to answer her and, as he did, he heard the cupboard door slam shut and then lock from the inside. But not before he'd seen a pair of gleaming yellow eyes peering out at him through the darkness.

A bead of sweat trickled down the length of Stanley's back. He'd been mistaken – it wasn't some*one* hiding in that cupboard. It was some*thing*.

Chapter Four
The Cupboard Under the Stairs

Stanley's eyeballs were bulging so far out of their sockets they seemed in danger of shooting clean across the carpet. He was breathing so fast, sucking in so much air, he feared his head might explode like an overinflated football. Never, not even when Justin Gudgey had offered to perform plastic surgery on him with a blowtorch in DT, had he been so terrified.

Staring at the cupboard door, Stanley racked his brain for an explanation of what he'd just seen. There just wasn't one. Something was in there; he knew that for a fact. Something that was sitting just inches away from him, probably plotting its next devious move.

Struggling to listen over the racket of his pounding heart, he leaned further towards the cupboard door, but he couldn't hear anything inside. The only sound came from Mum, laughing as she watched him from the top of the stairs.

'Stanley, what exactly are you doing?'

How could he reply when his imagination had rocketed into maximum overdrive? *Something evil is in there,* a voice echoed in his ears. *A thing that's been watching you; following you about...* He paused, shuddering as the image of those wicked yellow eyes danced in his brain. *Something that can't possibly be* – he whispered the next word out loud: 'human.'

'Stanley, did you hear me?' Mum was on the bottom stair now, frustration arching her eyebrows. 'It's a cupboard. We have them in London, too, remember?'

Stanley looked up at her expectant face. It would be pointless telling her what he'd just seen; she would never believe him. There was more chance of growing a beard bigger than Dad's in the next three minutes than convincing Mum that something weird and wicked was hiding out in the cupboard under the stairs.

Directing his eyes back towards the creature's lair, Stanley took a long, steadying breath, trying to keep his voice as light as possible when he said, 'Mum, do you have a key for this cupboard?'

She stepped past him into the living room. 'Your father has all the keys to this place,' she called out. 'You'd better ask him. If you can find him, that is.'

So that was it then, Stanley would have to wait here, in this exact position. He couldn't risk letting the creature out of his sight, even if it meant staying rooted to the spot for the entire summer. But wait a minute, he scanned the wood and gasped; this door didn't have a keyhole either.

A sudden smash of china echoed from the living room. 'Oh, for goodness sake,' Mum cried out. '*That* wasn't there earlier. Who's been moving things around in here?'

Stanley could hear Mum's angry footsteps stomping in his direction. Luckily, her attention was fixed on her missing husband. '*Will*, where *are* you?'

There was no reply.

'What's all the shouting about?' Scarlett was glaring down from the balcony. 'I thought you dragged us to the cruddy countryside for some peace and quiet.'

Mum glared up at Scarlett with blotches of what looked like her homemade trifle spreading over her cheeks. 'Where would you like me to start?' she said, her tone dangerous. Mum's patience had clearly run out and this wasn't going to be pretty.

'Let's see, shall we – it appears we've rented a house more reminiscent of a festering flea market. A place so crammed with clutter we don't stand a chance of unpacking. The owners are less contactable than the Prime Minister, so I have no idea why it's all still here, and I'm getting no help from either of you.' She glared at both twins, her brilliant blue eyes flashing. 'I have a daughter who seems to think this house is only made up of her bedroom, a son who thinks the same about a cupboard, and a husband,' she was yelling now, 'a husband who seems more dedicated to moving into the garden shed than in here! And what is more –'

Stanley's head shrunk into his shoulders ready for the oncoming explosion. But it didn't come from Mum. Her jaw snapped shut as all three of them stared in disbelief at Stanley's cupboard.

From the crashing and thudding now coming from behind the door, it sounded like a blindfolded rhinoceros was loose in there.

Mum gripped Stanley's shoulder, pulling him backwards. He glanced up at Scarlett, who was standing open-mouthed and, for the second time that day, speechless.

The cupboard's brass door handle began to rattle furiously: whatever was in there was trying to get out. Then came a loud pounding and with every thud the door loosened further off its hinges.

'Out the front door, *now!*' Mum beckoned to Scarlett with one hand, her grip on Stanley's shoulder tightening with the other.

They'd only made it halfway towards the front doors when the hallway was filled with an almighty bellowing and the cupboard door flew off its hinges, narrowly missing Stanley's head on its way past him. An explosion of dust burst from the entrance as a massive figure emerged, headfirst and coughing like a ten-a-day pipe smoker.

Dad wiped the dirt from his eyes and plucked a dead spider out of his beard. Clearing his throat, he beamed at his flabbergasted family.

'You'll never believe what I've just found in there,' he said.

Chapter Five

Beetles and Bones

Dad leapt towards Stanley, hauling him through the now empty doorway before anyone had time to peel the dust from their eyelashes.

'Come back!' Mum yelled.

'Won't be a jiffy, Nelly,' Dad called back, shoving the broken door into place behind them. 'We can't let your mum see what's down here,' he whispered. 'She'll lock it all up and swallow the key.'

Somehow Stanley doubted that. More likely, Dad had found something he wasn't ready to share with too many, too soon. Stanley smiled to himself, happy that Dad had chosen him to share his secrets with.

There was a rattling noise, then a few muffled swearwords from Dad. The torchlight flickered on and off, eventually leaving them in darkness.

'Ruddy batteries must've gone,' Dad moaned. 'Just hold on to me.' He shuffled around, walking slowly forwards. 'The tunnel's going to get pretty narrow, so stay close.'

Something dank clung to Stanley's nostrils and dive-bombed his throat as they scrambled and crouched their way along the tunnel. He stuffed his nose and mouth into one of his sleeves to mask the smell, the other arm clumsily grabbing at Dad's back. It was blacker than a winter midnight in here and Stanley expected to see those beady yellow eyes piercing the darkness at any moment.

It wasn't long before the tunnel began to feel warm and soon a ruby light appeared, bleeding through the dark air towards them. Dad stopped suddenly, causing Stanley to taste a mouthful of his knitted tank top. It had the faint flavour of Marmite.

'We're here,' said Dad, his outline illuminated in the flickering glow.

Stanley jumped backwards when he saw what Dad was pointing at. They were standing on the edge of a narrow opening, flames licking the air below their feet.

'Why is there a *fire d*own there?' Stanley exclaimed.

'Trust me,' Dad replied, grinning, as he lowered himself down. His feet landed heavily on the floor below, leaving only his top half poking up through the gap. 'Come on then,' he said with a wink, lifting Stanley down. 'You're going to love this.'

A moment later Stanley found himself standing beside Dad inside a giant stone fireplace, having just emerged from the chimney flue above. With relief, he saw that the fire itself was contained inside an iron grate.

'Pretty nifty, eh,' said Dad. 'Why should Santa Claus be the only one who gets to climb up and down chimneys?'

Stanley's eyes moved from the crackling fire to the many lamps casting their orange glow over the room; Dad had clearly been making himself at home down here.

'What is this place?' Stanley asked, coughing slightly. The air was a heady mixture of smoke and chemicals.

'I'm guessing it used to be a priest hole,' Dad replied. 'You know what they are, right?' He sighed at the blank look on Stanley's face. 'Being a Catholic in England could get you into a lot of trouble at one time,' Dad went on, 'so hidden rooms and chapels were built inside these big houses.'

'Oh, yeah, we did this at school,' Stanley exclaimed. 'They used to hide the entrances to priest holes behind panels in the walls or inside staircases, even under those old wooden toilets.' His stomach squirmed at the thought.

'That's right,' Dad said. 'Then the important, secret, Catholic families could hold Mass and, even if the house was searched the priest-hunters wouldn't be able to find them.' Dad's eyes shone with excitement. 'But I found a way in,' he said, gesturing to a small door on the opposite side of room. 'There's a tunnel through there that leads into the garden shed. Can you believe there was a trap door in the shed, hidden under a massive pile of manure?'

But Stanley's eyes were glued to the chimney. 'How did you know there was another entrance *up there?*'

'I didn't,' said Dad. 'I looked up when I lit the fire, and *Hey Presto!* There it was.'

'This room's not a priest hole now though, is it,' Stanley said, his eyes not able to rest on any one thing as they flew around the room. 'It looks more like some kind of laboratory.'

And he was right. In front of them was an assortment of old fashioned weighing scales, and other gadgets Stanley didn't recognise. Next to these were phials and beakers, some of them smashed, drops of colourful liquids still clinging to the cracked glass.

'Why are these broken?' Stanley asked, twirling a test tube in his fingers.

'Well, I haven't been dancing on the tables,' Dad laughed. 'Who knows, I suppose Archibald Marble was getting a bit clumsy in his old age.'

'Is that who owns the house?' Stanley said. 'You haven't told us anything about him.'

'That's because I don't know much,' Dad replied, scratching his beard. 'He's an old man who's gone abroad for his health; that's about all his niece and nephew told us. They're renting out the house for him while he's away. A right odd pair they are too.'

'When did you meet them?' Stanley asked, feeling chilly all of a sudden.

'They came to see us in London last month.' Dad's eyes slipped past Stanley to a tall set of shelves on the back wall. 'Came to check us out, I suppose; make sure we weren't a family of weirdos before they let us rent the place.' He turned back to Stanley. 'They asked to meet you and Scarlett, but your mum palmed them off with some photos. Shame you were at school, they were a sight to behold.' Laughing at the memory, Dad moved towards the shelves, reaching for a jar filled to the brim with what looked like dead slugs. 'Wonder what these are for?' he said, thoughtfully, lifting off the lid and sniffing the contents.

The shelves were packed with corked glass bottles that tinkled when Dad ran his giant hands over them. Their labels were smudged, making it hard to read the words on them, but moving closer, Stanley could make out a few – *Elder Essence, Powdered Mugwort, Devil's Claw, Agrimony Root*. He had no idea what any of these things were. There were books too and he ran his hand over their peeling spines, reading the titles aloud – '*The Kiss of the Deathstalker, Amicus Venenum, Myth & Mammalia...*'

A large and tattered book lay discarded on the floor. Its cover was made of thick dark leather and showed engraved patterns swirling inside rows of squares. Stanley bent down to pick it up. He had never seen a book like this one before.

Heaving it open he found its pages to be made of a smooth, cloth-like material, the words and illustrations painted onto them in faded inks. The pages were covered with detailed drawings of plants and animals. On one a long blue and orange lizard coiled its tail around words written in an unfamiliar language.

'Dad, have you seen this?'

Stanley heard a low whistle behind him, Dad grabbing the book and slowly turning the pages. 'I – I don't believe it; it's a *Leechbook*. Look at the writing, Stanley; it's Old English.' Dad was handling the book like it was something rare and precious. 'There can't be many original manuscripts like this around.' His forehead furrowed. 'I've only ever seen one at the university.'

The last thing Stanley had wanted was to remind Dad about losing his job. To distract him, Stanley said, 'What's a Leechbook, when it's at home?'

This made Dad chuckle. 'It's an ancient book of healing; Anglo Saxon. Just look at the plant cures in here.' He began translating the pages, 'An *Elder Root Elixir* for coughs and bronchitis… a *Poultice of Comfrey* for wounds that won't heal… *Mugwort Tea* for feelings of unease.'

Stanley bit into his lip; he could do with a cup of Mugwort tea right now. 'So if this book was Archibald Marble's, does that mean the old man was some kind of doctor?'

'That's what I'd like to know,' said Dad, handing the book carefully back to Stanley. He'd spotted a huge glass-fronted cabinet, its doors hanging open.

Stanley looked down at the plant drawings on the open page. 'It would make sense if Mr Marble was some kind of herbal doctor, like that bloke on the telly,' he said. 'He's got a massive greenhouse.' And now Stanley came to think of it, there was a hint of that sweet greenhouse smell in the air down here too.

'Maybe Mr Marble brought the plants down here to make his medicines?' he exclaimed, pulling in a long deep sniff and wishing suddenly that he hadn't breathed. There was something sickly and clinging about the smell; fragrant on the surface but cloying underneath, like the smell of the bathroom after Dad had been in there – a mixture of Dad's bum and air freshener. Coughing, Stanley remembered Aunt Ada's herbal remedies, the teas she used to make them drink

41

that smelled of old socks. He shuddered, he wouldn't be rushing to learn any of Archibald Marble's recipes, however keen Dad might be.

Stanley moved to join Dad at the cabinet. Inside was a shelf of perfectly intact snakeskins, weaving their way around glass pots filled to the brim with dead beetles and spiders. Another shelf held at least twenty screw top jars, their contents impossible to make out inside strange murky liquids. And there was a collection of small skeletons and skulls; some of the skulls with large teeth that looked more like fangs. Something inside Stanley began hotting up.

'Maybe old Marble was a vet,' Dad mused, brandishing a jar with a tiny brain floating in it.

'A vet!' Stanley stared at the fanged skulls. 'Where? At Hogwarts?'

'Move aside, Dr Doolittle, here comes Dr Doolally,' Dad guffawed.

As Stanley peered further into the cabinet, his stomach felt like a slab of butter dissolving slowly in the microwave. Right in the middle sat the skeleton of an enormous foot, its thick, many-jointed toes gripping the edge of a shelf.

'What is *that?*'

Dad poked his head so far into the cabinet it looked like the skeleton toes were clawing his beard.

'Hmm, upon closer inspection,' said Dad, heaving himself back out, 'I would say that those toes once belonged to Bigfoot.'

Stanley couldn't laugh. 'I'm serious, Dad. Don't you think this is getting too weird? The stuff down here makes the rest of the house look almost normal. It doesn't make any sense.'

'Does it have to?' Dad laid his hand on Stanley's shoulder. 'Maybe Archibald Marble is some kind of doctor, or even a vet. Or *maybe* he just likes buying crazy things in his spare time.' Dad gave Stanley one of his rare serious looks. 'Listen, son, not everyone in this life fits into a neat box, and the world would be a pretty boring place if they did, don't you agree?' He winked, reaching into his pocket and pulling out something small in red velvet. 'Talking of boxes, look what I found.'

It was a ring box that held an eye in place of a ring. 'I'm guessing it's glass,' Dad chuckled, 'before you get any ghoulish ideas.'

The eye stared out of the box, its glass iris glistening, and a jolt of electricity catapulted Stanley's stomach halfway up his windpipe. It had reminded him of *the creature*. For a tiny, wonderful, moment, he'd forgotten all about that thing. For all he knew it could be watching them at this very moment, skulking among the shadows.

'Can we go back upstairs now?' Stanley asked, fighting to stop the wobble in his voice.

Dad ruffled his hair. 'Come on then,' he sighed. 'Let's get a take-away in before your mum tries to cook.'

Chapter Six
An Extraordinary Dinner Party

It was almost nine o'clock that evening when Stanley sat silently in the window seat of his bedroom, staring down at the moonlit garden. A summer breeze was dancing through the trees, making ghost-like shadows among the shivering branches. Out of all the places his parents could have chosen for a holiday, he thought with a shudder, why did they have to choose here? And for the entire summer too.

The cushion beneath him was lumpy and he shifted forward to a more comfy patch. It was then that he saw it: a small shape moving through the garden. It was an animal, trotting back and forth across the grass, sniffing the ground. Stanley narrowed his eyes, his nose touching the glass in an attempt to see better. The animal had a long bushy tail – a fox. It was darting here and there, turning in circles and sniffing the ground. It moved to the edge of the garden and a moment later was gone, swallowed by the forest trees.

Stanley's gaze travelled back into his bedroom. The smallest room in the house, it was still much bigger than his bedroom at home. If his friends could see the crooked furniture, the flowery bedspread and matching wallpaper, he'd never live it down. He jumped up. Well, there was something he could do about that at least.

Yanking a roll of football posters from the pile of stuff on his bed, Stanley pinned every one of them to the walls. He was halfway through swapping pink roses for his Thor bedspread, when Mum's head peered around the door.

'The food's *finally* arrived,' she said. 'No easy task getting a take-away delivered out here.' She winked. 'Although I doubt cooking in that kitchen will be much easier.'

It hardly seemed possible, but once Stanley had sat down at the gigantic dinner table, his unease about this house, even his fear of the yellow-eyed creature, was chased from his belly by the grumbling hunger in there.

'Do we have to wait for Scarlett?' he said, eyeing the silver cartons Mum was unpacking. 'I'm starving.'

'Come on, Stanley,' Mum said, 'it'll be nice for us all to eat together.' She glanced over at Dad, who was also sat at the table, bushy head buried in a book with a unicorn on the cover. 'And that includes you, Will.'

Dad didn't seem to hear her and continued reading, 'Oohing' and 'Ahhing' every few seconds.

Stanley was about to sneak a poppadom, when the air was pierced by a scream from somewhere upstairs.

'Scarlett!' Mum gasped, knocking over the mango chutney

in her race to flee the room.

Stanley's insides shriveled when he imagined what Scarlett might have found up there, but after what he'd seen in that cupboard he had to know. With a slow, shaky breath, he tiptoed after them.

Creeping along the first floor landing, Stanley arrived at Scarlett's bedroom and pressed his ear against the door.

'What were you thinking?' Mum was asking over Scarlett's muffled sobs. 'Where did you get it from? Oh, the smell.'

Then came Scarlett's strangely small voice, 'It was your f–face pack, Mum.'

'What are you on about?' Mum replied, a shocked kind of laughter ringing through her voice. 'I don't have a face-pack made of... well, it can only be... *horse manure*.'

'*What?*' This was the last thing Stanley had expected to hear. He shoved the door open to find Scarlett slumped on the bed, her miserable face dripping with stinking brown gunge.

Stanley would normally have laughed himself silly at the sight of Scarlett covered in horse poo, but here, in this house, a shadowy fear passed through him instead. Staring at his sobbing sister, all words stuck fast to his lips.

There wasn't much Scarlett could say either, not without sucking in great lumps of the stuff, and she leapt up suddenly, tears streaking the muck on her face as she ran from the room. Passing him on her way to the bathroom, Scarlett threw Stanley a look that sent a shiver through him. There had been shame in her eyes, no doubt, but it was terror that shone brightest.

'Go and have your dinner, Stanley,' Mum said. 'We'll be down in a minute.'

Food the last thing on his mind right now, he gripped the bannister, making his way slowly downstairs. *Five weeks they had to stay in this house, five long weeks.*

Stanley wasn't sure how he reached the dining room, but when he did he was snapped out of his fearful daze at the sight of Dad, who was in fits of laughter, prodding his savaloy-sized fingers into the cartons of curry.

'Great joke, son, I'm guessing you swiped these from the priest hole?' Dad plucked something brightly coloured from one of the curry cartons, holding it up to his face. 'Purple centipedes, eh. Now, where did old Archie find these, I wonder?'

'Dad, I don't know what you're talk–' The end of the sentence dissolved on Stanley's tongue. Peering into the carton, he goggled at the rainbow of crinkly insects floating amidst a gloopy orange sauce.

'Best get rid of 'em before the women folk get down here,' Dad said, dropping his voice theatrically. 'The fuss they'd make about this lot. Where did you put the real food, son?'

Stanley's lips could only flap like a stranded sardine when he tried to reply.

Dad chuckled, bounding out of the room. 'I need the lav,' he called back. 'You've got five minutes to return my Vindaloo.'

'Right.' Mum had appeared in the doorway. She sat down at the table. 'That really wasn't funny, Stanley.'

'What? I didn't make that face pack!' Stanley was indignant. 'Where would I find horse manure?'

'If I had to guess, I'd say the greenhouse,' Mum replied, stiffly. 'Don't you think I've got enough to deal with at the moment?'

Stanley was about to argue with this unfair statement, but was quickly distracted by the contaminated food cartons staring up at him. Mum must have seen the look of panic on his face because she said, more kindly, 'Let's just forget about it now. I know this place isn't quite what we promised, but there'll be some fun things for us to do, I promise.'

'Mum, I…'

'Ah, Cornelia, you're here.' Dad was back, rubbing his round belly. 'I trust we're ready to commence our exotic feast?' He gave Stanley a sly wink and tiptoed to the table. 'All as it should be then, young son of mine?'

Breathing fast, Stanley glanced from Dad to Mum and back again. What was going on here? Surely Dad was double bluffing him; he *had* to be the one behind all this.

'Where's the prawn Korma?' Mum asked, reaching a hand towards one of the cartons. Stanley could barely look when she raised a plump pink specimen to her lips and began to chew.

'Aaooooowwww! What is *that*?' Mum coughed into a napkin and stared at the chewed up insect in her hand, her eyes throbbing like saucers behind her glasses.

At that moment Scarlett walked into the room. Her gaze fell on the insect stew in Mum's open hand, and for a brief second a smile flickered over her lips. 'Er, Mum, what are you eating?'

Mum had spotted Scarlett's smile. '*You* did this?'

'*What* did I do?' Scarlett looked at each of them in turn.

'I don't know if you're trying to play tricks on each other, or on me, but I've just about had enough.' Tears sprung into

Mum's eyes. 'And if I find *you've* had anything to do with this, Will.'

'I most certainly have *not*, Madam!' Dad exclaimed, dropping the poppadom he'd been using to scratch an eyebrow. 'You've seen me reading in here all evening.' He pulled Mum into a cuddle, his voice softening. 'Come on, Nelly, it's all just high spirits. I'm sure they're both very sorry, right kids?' He stared at the twins expectantly.

Stanley watched Scarlett's expression. It was angry and bewildered, but not guilty.

'It's late, I think you should both go to bed,' said Mum.

'But, I –' Stanley began, but Mum's face was determined.

'*Now*,' she said, turning away before either of them could argue further.

Together, they climbed the stairs, where Scarlett stopped, turning around to face Stanley. 'We both know I had nothing to do with any of that,' she said, 'and if this was your way of trying to convince Mum and Dad there's something creepy in this house…'

The threat hung in the air between them.

'It wasn't me, Scarlett,' Stanley replied quietly, climbing onto the same step as her so that their eyes were level. 'Honestly, I've got no clue about what just happened.'

For a tiny moment something like fear flashed across Scarlett's face. Then she hesitated, shaking her head. 'Yeah, right,' she said, turning away from him and running up the last of the stairs. She disappeared, slamming her bedroom door behind her.

Chapter Seven

Beloved Bella

Next day was better. The heaviness of the house had lifted from Stanley's shoulders the moment his family left its groaning gates; walking together into the village and hiring bikes from the little repair shop on the green.

For miles they cycled along endless winding lanes, among hills and fields blanketed with silken poppies and creamy buttercups, eventually taking a craggy path toward the sea cliffs. Even Scarlett managed to forget her anger at Stanley as they chased each other along.

'Be careful, you two,' Dad called out.

The twins almost collided in their sudden halt, laughing as

they made their way back towards Mum and Dad, who were now sitting on a rock, unpacking lunch.

'Not a Barghest in sight,' Mum chuckled, winking at the twins. Stanley took his sandwich from her with a smirk, but he couldn't help shooting a tentative glance at the distant craggy hills.

Picking up a flat stone, Scarlett ran her hands over its smooth surface thoughtfully. 'Did anyone work out who the stone statue in the dining room is yet?'

'Ah, our hero healer,' Dad said. 'Haven't you two just been studying Greek Mythology at school? I'd have thought you'd've recognised him straight away.'

Stanley thought back to his schoolbooks at home, his mind running over their picture-filled pages. 'Of course, Asclepius!' he exclaimed. 'The Greek God of medicine.'

'That's right,' Mum said. 'A snake licked Asclepius' ears clean and whispered secret knowledge into them.'

Dad laughed at Scarlett's shudder. 'It was well worth that snake's tongue in old Asclepius' ear; he could bring people back to life from the brink of death, and beyond.'

'Actually,' Mum said now, 'animals are sacred beings of wisdom and healing in many cultures. Often acting as guardians, they –'

'Mum, we're on *holiday*,' Scarlett groaned. 'Don't start with the school stuff, you both promised.'

Stanley threw Scarlett a sideways grin, but he'd been secretly enjoying Mum's words.

Enfolding Mum in a squeeze, Dad pointed suddenly upwards to where a great bird was souring above them on grey brown wings. 'Look, Nelly, a golden eagle. A rare sight in

England, what a treat.' He glanced back at the twins, an eyebrow flickering. 'Eagles are believed by the Celts to possess powerful magical knowledge and to only reveal that knowledge to the worthy.'

'Let's see if we can catch it, then.' Scarlett leapt onto her bike. 'Come on Stanley.'

It was many hours, and endless miles of cycling, later that they arrived back at the house. The sun, low and red in the sky, threw a rich, comforting glow over the grounds and a soft breeze made it feel like being bathed in velvet. For the first time since they'd arrived here, Stanley felt less afraid of Marble Manor.

'Dinner in an hour, kids,' Dad called, as he and Mum disappeared inside with the shopping.

'I've got an idea,' Scarlett said, her eyes shining. 'Let's see if we can get a peek into the east wing. Why d'you think it's locked up?'

'Mr Marble never uses it, it's too run down,' Stanley replied simply. 'That's what Mum said anyway.'

'Or *maybe* it's because there's even weirder stuff in there, or something *hidden,* that we're not meant to see.' She grabbed Stanley's arm. 'Come on, don't say you're scared.'

'I'm not,' he replied, beaming when he realised this was the truth. 'Let's go.'

As if to avoid the eyes of the stone gargoyles, which looked like they might swoop down on them from the roof at any moment, the twins crept through the wild grass towards the right hand side of the house. Here they tiptoed up to each of the front windows in turn, silently peering inside. To their disappointment, every windowpane was dark and they could only see cracked wood behind the glass.

'Looks like closed shutters,' Stanley said. 'I can't see anything inside.'

So they made their way around the side of the house, only to discover the same thing: nothing. All the windows were either guarded by shutters or hung with heavy curtains, making it impossible to see anything at all of the east wing.

What they did discover was an ornate garden full of rose bushes and little brick pathways that lead to a pond with a stone fountain in the middle of it. Both were dry and the two dancing mermaids holding the bowl of the fountain were a marble of moss.

A wrought iron table and chair sat half hidden among browning roses, and when Stanley moved closer he saw a single teacup and saucer filled with rainwater. A snail clung to a book, its silvery trail twirling over the leather cover like the words of a strange language. It made Stanley think of Archibald's Leechbook.

'Stanley, *quick;* come and see this.'

Scarlett's voice reached him from outside the rose garden, through an archway on its far side. Here, Stanley found her pointing towards the edge of the grounds, where thick tree roots slivered through the unruly grass. His eyes followed her pointing finger to a group of stone slabs.

'I think they're graves,' she whispered, a slight shudder in her voice.

Moving wordlessly together, they felt for each other's hands as they came to the edge of the garden.

The graves wove in uneven lines through forest shadows. Each headstone belonged to a Marble, dating back hundreds of years. That is, all except one. This one belonged to someone named only as *Beloved Bella*. Whoever Bella was, Stanley worked out, she had died thirty years ago, much more recently than the others. A bunch of dead roses lay on her grave, their dry petals still prettily pink.

'Bit creepy burying your family in the garden,' Scarlett said, 'however big it is.' But Stanley's attention was on something else. Moving closer to one of the graves, he ran his fingers over a symbol set deep into the stone. It was a series of overlaying circles and triangles that made him think of mountains and moons. As he looked around he saw that the symbol was on every stone. Every stone except Bella's.

'I wonder what it means?' he whispered.

Scarlett shrugged. 'Who knows, it's probably like everything else around here, completely bonkers.'

'Stanley laughed. 'I s'pose, but why doesn't Bella have one of these symbols on her grave?'

'Hers doesn't say Marble, does it?' Scarlett answered. 'Maybe she wasn't part of the family.' She giggled. 'Maybe she was Archibald's girlfriend.'

Somehow Stanley didn't feel like laughing this time. Just at that moment a cool breeze blew over them, lifting the fallen leaves from the graves and rustling the branches of the trees. The breeze carried a smell with it, like something overripe. Stanley's eyes wandered over the roses on Bella's grave and towards the rose garden; all those browning petals heated by the hot summer air to create a strange layer of smells, both sweet and sour.

He moved towards the forest, its promise of fresh bark and living leaves calling on his senses. But as he stepped closer, the horrible smell only grew stronger, like it wasn't coming from the rose garden at all, but from the forest itself.

'What is it?' Scarlett asked, her nose ruffling.

Stanley didn't know, and suddenly he didn't want to either. He didn't want to know anything about the bad smell, about the graves, or about what might be hidden in the east wing. His fear was back, scratching at his skin like it wanted to climb inside him and live there forever. He couldn't let that happen. He *wouldn't*. He needed to be near his dad, to smell his Marmitey smell, and to be wrapped in the safety of his laughter.

'Sorry,' Stanley murmured, before turning away from Scarlett and running as fast as he could back towards the house.

Chapter Eight

The Speakers of Ancient Tongues

'You have to wonder why Archibald Marble collected fire beetle wings.' Dad was sitting on the sofa, reading out the labels from the jars he'd brought out of the priest hole yesterday. 'And look at these yellow slugs, they're massive!' He waved a large and shrivelled specimen under the twins' noses.

Scarlett peered at the dead creature in Dad's hand. 'Maybe Mr Marble was trying some French style recipes,' she said. 'You know, French people cook snails, so why shouldn't he do the same with slugs? Or maybe we should ask Stanley.' She glared at him suddenly. 'He seems good at cooking with disgusting ingredients.'

Stanley didn't answer. His attention had been caught by the stuffed fox, which was now lying on the back of the sofa. He wasn't one hundred percent certain, but he could've sworn the fox's face had been pointing in the other direction the last time he'd seen it.

'Dad, did you bring that thing in here?' he asked.

'Don't change the subject,' Scarlett snapped at Stanley, her cheeks glowing. 'Just admit all that stuff the other night was you, and apologise.'

'Not this again,' Stanley replied, anger forcing his face towards hers. 'How could I have cooked up curried insects without any of you seeing? Or carried horse manure through the house without you smelling it? Dad, tell her you didn't see me do anything!'

But Dad appeared to be lost in thought and, raising an eyebrow, he popped a slug into his mouth. The twins grimaced as Dad chewed the slug without flinching, savouring the flavour of the dissolving mollusc. 'Mmmm, tastes like your mum's savoury chutney,' he said, smacking his lips together.

Stanley couldn't help wondering at Dad's amused expression. If he could sit there happily munching on a dead slug, then why should Stanley be surprised if it *was* Dad who'd set up the insect curry, and even the face pack? It was true that Dad was usually proud of his joke playing, but maybe there was a reason he hadn't come clean yet. On the other hand, Dad wouldn't have let them go without dinner because of his own joke. Was he saying no more about last night because he thought, like the others, that Stanley was behind it all?

There was no more time to think about it; Marble Manor's

out-of-tune doorbell had just clanged through the living room. They all listened, Dad continuing to pick lumps of slug from between his teeth. The front door opened and a murmur of voices seeped in from the hallway.

'So enraptured to see you again, my dear Mrs Crankshaw,' a man's voice sang. His cut glass accent would've made Stanley's headmaster proud. 'Although my sister and I would never dream of disturbing you, so you simply must tell us if we're intruding.'

Stanley heard quiet laughter from another person he assumed was the sister. Then Mum's much more sheepish voice, 'Not at all... please, come in.'

Giving a great gasp, Stanley almost swallowed a passing moth. An enormously fat man had stepped through the doorway after Mum. Hardly dressed for summer, his chunky body parts were wedged into a three-piece checked suit, with a thick-collared shirt and tie. Although handsome, the man's pale face wore a pinched expression, and a curling black moustache – surely a distraction from his combed-over hair – framed a tight mouth. Stanley considered him for a long moment; for someone so fat, his face wasn't quite right. He looked like a skinny man peering over a giant sack of potatoes.

Now he manoeuvred towards the sofa, completely unaware when his oversized bum knocked over a lamp. 'Ah, the children,' he said, beaming at the twins before reaching out beefy arms to Scarlett and taking her hand in his.

'This is Aleister and Lyla Cabell,' said Mum, gesturing to a slender woman, who had also stepped into the room. 'Mr Archibald Marble's niece and nephew.'

'Such a pleasure to see you all,' the woman said. Her voice

was warm and soft, like a cat's belly. Unlike her brother, Lyla Cabell was a picture of elegance. Curled raven black hair framed the delicate features of her face, her slim frame bathed in black satin.

Stanley didn't quite like the fact that, like him and Scarlett, the Cabells had black hair and blue eyes. Yet, while Aleister's hair was thin and wispy, his silvery blue eyes surrounded by shadows; Lyla's hair was thick and lustrous, and she regarded each of them in turn with eyes like shimmering sapphires.

A butterfly fluttered in Stanley's stomach when she stepped closer. Then a moment later he felt his nose scrunching; her perfume was so overpowering it made him feel quite sick. Slowly, he edged away from her; it seemed there was little to like about either Cabell.

'Don't worry about *him*,' Scarlett whispered loudly, pulling her hand free of Aleister and nodding towards Stanley. 'He's always scared of strangers.'

There was no time for Stanley to protest at this: Aleister Cabell had grabbed his hand, and was soon shaking it with the force of a champion wrestler. Stanley glanced at the hand gripping his own; it was bony, not an inch of fat on it.

'Such a pleasure to meet you,' Aleister Cabell said, staring at Stanley for an uncomfortably long time. Stanley tried to release his hand but the man's fingers had locked around it. A moment later they began to tremble.

'Are you okay, Mr Cabell?' Stanley asked, just as the hand twitched open again.

'Oh, call me Aleister,' he said, spinning away from Stanley, and acting as though he hadn't heard the question. 'So how are you all settling in? Must be a delightful change from smoggy old London.'

Dad moved to the large fireplace, where he leaned against the mantelpiece, peering down at these uninvited visitors from his lofty height. 'We'd quite like to know why none of your uncle's things have been cleared away,' he said. 'My wife has tried to call you countless times.'

'Oh, yes, I *am* sorry,' Aleister said with his thin smile. 'We've been away, you see, and I'll be honest, there's been a delay in getting things moved. We've mislaid something quite special and we really do need to find it first.'

'That's right,' Lyla chimed in, her long-lashed gaze flitting around the room. 'We couldn't risk letting the cleaners in here, not until it's been found. Heaven knows where it would end up.'

Stanley watched Lyla's smile settle into the milk-white skin of her face. Away from her dodgy perfume she really was quite beautiful.

'And you couldn't have told us this before we arrived?' Dad asked, with more than a hint of impatience.

Lyla's smile faded and something cruel took over her face instead. It seemed to be pushing its way out from inside, distorting her beauty. Then she blinked and it was gone.

Mum coughed. 'So what is it you're looking for? Perhaps we've seen it.'

'Ah, a most cherished family heirloom,' Aleister sighed. 'Uncle Archie would never forgive us if anything happened to it.'

'Where is Mr Marble?' Stanley piped up. 'He must have left in a hurry. Scarlett found his false teeth yesterday.'

'Ah, yes, alas, dear old Uncle is somewhat poorly,' Aleister said, stepping towards a row of portraits on the wall. He gestured to one of an old man with an unruly mop of white hair and a pair of keen amber eyes that smiled from behind round spectacles.

'That portrait was painted just before his illness,' Aleister said, shaking his tiny head and giving a dry sniff. 'Uncle Archie has gone to a clinic in Switzerland, where they specialise in...' He hesitated for a moment. 'His type of... problem.'

'The treatment is rather expensive,' Lyla added with a sad smile. 'That's why we are renting the manor out for him. Every penny helps.'

When Dad cleared his throat, Mum said hurriedly, 'We do appreciate the very good deal you gave us.'

'Say nothing of it, my dear,' Aleister simpered, waving his flabby arms around the room. 'Uncle has certainly struggled to maintain the Manor's former glory, so we could hardly charge a high rent for the place.'

'What kind of heirloom are you looking for, Mr Cabell?' Scarlett asked, Mum smiling her thanks at the change of subject.

'A very special book, my dear,' Lyla said, her eyes glittering. 'Hundreds of years old and of great value; historical of course. It is most beloved by Uncle Archie and we simply must find it.'

'It's mostly in old languages, so it wouldn't make much sense to *you*,' said Aleister. 'Whereas Uncle Archie taught us the ancient tongues when we were children.' He puffed out his mountainous chest.

Dad twitched an eyebrow. '*Possum loqui variis linguis,*' he said.

'You speak Latin?' said Aleister with some astonishment. '*Admirabilis.*'

'Anglo-Saxon too,' Dad smiled, 'and some Greek and Aramaic.'

Lyla glided towards Dad like a beautiful ghost. 'So you're a man of letters, Willard,' she said, gazing up at him. 'What a wonderful thing to pass onto your children. Didn't I say they'd be perfect for the place, Aleister?' She purred, not taking her eyes from Dad's, 'We interviewed a great many familes, Willard, but I knew as soon as we met, that yours would be just the right *match.*'

Mum moved to place herself between Dad and Lyla. '*My husband* is an archaeologist and *I'm* an anthropologist,' she said. 'Until recently we both worked at the University of –'

'I'm sure they don't want to hear our CVs, Cornelia,' Dad interrupted. He glared at both Cabells in turn. 'I'm afraid we haven't seen your book.'

'You're quite sure you've not stumbled across anything *promising?*' Lyla asked coyly, tilting her head at Dad.

Stanley thought about the Leechbook; surely this was what the Cabells were after. One glimpse of Dad's face kept him quiet on the subject. Dad had clearly taken a dislike to Archibald Marble's relatives, and Stanley couldn't agree with him more.

Aleister gave a reluctant sigh. 'Right, well, we best leave you to your unpacking. If you could just keep an eye out for the book, we'll get Archie's things moved into the east wing as soon as we've got it.'

'Is there no way you could move them sooner?' Mum

sounded tired. 'What if we can't find this book?'

'Oh, it's not so bad in here, is it, Cornelia?' Dad said suddenly. 'I'm actually getting quite used to it. The old man's belongings give the place a bit of... atmosphere.'

Mum's mouth fell open. 'Well, I... I'm not sure, Will.'

'Let's just leave things as they are for now.' Dad pulled himself up to his fullest height, which was at least two heads taller than either Cabell. 'So there's no need for either of you to come back, we have everything we need.'

'Well, if you're sure, Mr Crankshaw,' said Aleister, his face somewhat puckered. 'But don't hesitate to call us for anything, *anything*, at all. We're only up the road.'

Lyla's glittering gaze made one last search of the room before the pair disappeared from sight.

'What a load of rubbish about a family heirloom,' Dad roared, once the front door had closed behind the Cabells. 'I bet they know damn well where that book is; they probably know every inch of this house. They're just using it as an excuse.'

'An excuse for what?' Mum asked, baffled.

'To delay moving the old man's stuff,' Dad replied. 'That way they can keep coming back, to check up on us. Well I'm not having it. Coming in here like they're so much better than us.' It was rare to see Dad this angry. 'There's no way I'm having those two stuck-up idiots landing on the doorstep every five minutes.'

'Is that what you think they were doing?' Scarlett said. 'Checking up on us?'

Dad sucked the air in through his nose with a noisy whistle. 'They know we're a bit hard up for cash,' he said, his skin glowing hot beneath his beard. 'Probably worried we'll steal things.'

Mum's face flushed. 'I don't think so, Will. They seemed completely genuine about the book.'

Scarlett nodded in agreement.

'There wasn't anything genuine about those two,' Stanley said in a quiet voice.

They all turned to look at him.

'Oh, here we go,' Scarlett laughed. 'Don't tell me, they're really aliens in human form, come to suck out our brains.'

'Don't be stupid,' said Stanley. 'I just got a bad feeling about them, that's all.'

'Yeah well, if we worried every time *you* got a bad feeling,' Scarlett snorted, 'we'd never leave the house.'

Chapter Nine

The Whispering Wall

That night Stanley fell into an uneasy sleep. Disturbing visions, smells and sounds swirled through his dreams, his skin tingling against sweat-soaked sheets.

A thud and a creak. Stanley twitched.

The low murmur of voices. He opened his eyes.

Another thud and this time a groan. Stanley sprang upright, shaking his head. He was alone in his bedroom and must've been dreaming. He tried to remember what he'd been dreaming about, but the details were hazy. On the other hand, the uneasy feeling he was left with was very real.

The bedroom door burst open and Dad's voice boomed into the room. 'I hope you're hungry, sunshine, I'm cooking up a feast this morning.'

Before Stanley could reply, Dad had grabbed him, launching him in one swift move, over his shoulder. 'I think I'd've made a first-class fireman,' Dad chuckled, marching out of the bedroom with Stanley dangling upside down like a hooked haddock.

In what seemed like only a few of Dad's giant strides later, they arrived in the kitchen, where Dad lowered Stanley to the floor with a grin. 'Nice to see you up.'

Stanley flopped into a chair at the table, grateful to be released from his nightmare. 'Where's everyone else?' he yawned.

'Mum's taken Scarlett to a farm,. Apparently they've got horses.' Dad scratched his head, staring into the fridge. 'I could've sworn there was a full carton of orange juice in here last night, and *hey*, who ate all the cake?' He turned back to Stanley. 'Have you and your sister been sneaking down for a midnight feast?'

Stanley shook his head, Dad raising an eyebrow at him as he chopped a mountain of tomato and onion, chucking them into a pan with chilli pepper. The smell was delicious, but there was a hollow feeling in Stanley's stomach that had little to do with hunger.

'As long as they don't expect *me* to go horse riding,' Dad mused. 'The length of my legs, I'd end up running at the same time.'

Stanley tried to smile but his face felt like stone. In fact his whole body was weighed down with a horrible fear. He watched Dad happily cooking the breakfast and wished he could be more like him; always laughing and joking, whatever was thrown at him.

But however much Stanley wanted to be like his dad, he had one very big problem – he couldn't see anything at all to laugh about. Marble Manor was too many kinds of weird to count, however much everyone else shrugged it off. True, there'd been no more sign of those yellow eyes, but that didn't mean he'd forgotten about them. Then there was that revolting face pack and the insect curry. And now, to top it all off, the Cabells.

Cutting up the omelette, Dad slapped two slices into rolls, passing one to Stanley, and plonking down in a chair opposite him. 'Don't even think about putting ketchup on that,' he said, his mouth already full. Dad swallowed, his expression sheepish all of a sudden. 'You are okay, aren't you, son?' he said. 'You've just seemed, a bit… I mean, is me being out of work worrying you?'

Stanley shook his head. He didn't quite know how to say what he was really worrying about. Was there a chance Dad would take him seriously, if he shared his fears about the Cabells?

'You do know it was budget cuts, right?' Dad went on. He looked away from Stanley, examining the table instead. 'I was good at my job and I'm looking for another one. It's just tough at the moment.'

'It's not *that*,' Stanley said quickly. 'I know it wasn't your fault, Dad. They've cancelled loads of really good clubs at school too.' He thought for a moment. 'Although I won't miss woodwork with Mr Figwort. His breath always smelled like farts.'

Dad smirked at this. 'We just have to tighten our belts for a bit. Your mum's still got her job and I've got loads of ideas for my book. I –'

'Dad, it's okay,' Stanley said. Was it helpful or selfish to talk about what was really bothering him? The embarrassment on Dad's face definitely called for a change of subject. Taking a deep breath, Stanley went for it. 'It's the Cabells,' he said. 'Can I talk to you about them?'

Dad flashed a grin. 'If you want to put me off my breakfast.'

'It's just, they… they gave me the creeps. It felt like they were up to something… I dunno… *dodgy.*'

Dad looked thoughtful. 'I'll admit they're an odd pair and I definitely don't relish being around them. But however clever they think they are, I wouldn't exactly put them in the Bond villain category.' He smiled kindly at Stanley. 'You've got to keep that imagination of yours in check, sunshine.'

'But –'

'Don't get me wrong,' Dad pressed, 'being imaginative is a gift, but you'll drive yourself bananas if you don't learn to tell the difference between reality and fiction. Just because people are irritating, it doesn't necessarily follow that they're up to something sinister. Okay?'

Stanley nodded, but the creeping dread in his stomach didn't agree.

'Now *Archibald Marble,* on the other hand,' said Dad, waving his fork excitedly at Stanley. A lump of eggy tomato flew off and landed on Stanley's pyjamas. 'Now he's my kind of fellow. This whole house is one giant treasure chest.'

Mum and Scarlett walked into the kitchen.

'Only a fellow hoarder of junk like *you* would think something like *that*,' Mum laughed, kissing Dad on the cheek before swiping his roll and taking a big bite. 'Aren't you going to make one for yourself?' she asked him, grinning.

Dad leaned back in his chair, a dreamy look coming over his face. 'Hoarder of junk indeed. I'll have you know that my collection of ear and nose hair trimmers was the envy of the Facial Hair Appreciation Society. Old Douggie Prudhoe himself said he'd never seen a more enviable array of hair-related machinery.'

'You're really not helping your case, Dad,' Scarlett giggled. 'Stanley, come and see the photos I took. There's a three-legged horse called Hilda at the farm who can still jump fences. They said we can ride her.'

Stanley allowed Scarlett to drag him from his chair and into the hallway, where something stopped him in his tracks. '*Wait... w*hat was that?' he said, pulling her back.

She turned to face him. 'What was what?'

'That noise, it came from... over *there*.' He pointed to the wall on the far side of the hallway.

'I can't hear –'

'Shhh,' Stanley hissed. He raced across the room, pressing his ear to the wall. There it was again – a shuffling, a scraping, and then – the murmur of... *voices*. Just like he'd heard in his bedroom!

'I wasn't dreaming! They're in *here*, Scarlett!' he cried, slapping the wall with the palm of his hand. 'Inside the walls.'

'What? *Who?* Don't tell me you're hearing things now.'

Stanley didn't answer. He was desperate to hear what the

voices were saying, but they had gone silent. The only sound was Scarlett's sighs as she waited for him to reply.

'It must've been something on the other side of the wall,' she reasoned, marching into the dining room.

'*What* exactly?' he replied, following close behind. 'Mum and Dad are in the kitchen, so who d'you think's in there?'

'Look, *there*!' Scarlett said, pointing at the dining room window. 'It's open, the wind was probably blowing through the room and *that's* the noise you heard.'

'What wind?' The curtains were still, not a hint of breeze moved them. 'I'm telling you, Scarlett, there were people *inside* that wall. I heard them in my bedroom too.'

Scarlett screwed her face up. 'Either this is another one of your wind-ups,' she said, marching out of the dining room. 'Or you're seriously round the twist. How can people fit inside walls?'

Stanley crossed the dining room unsteadily, collapsing into a chair at the big table and grabbing his face with both hands. He was so tired of it all – of being in this house, of being afraid, of feeling like he'd been singled out somehow; like he alone could see all the creepy things going on around here. Why would no one believe him?

Then a new and doubly horrifying thought slipped into his brain. What if his family was right? Was it all just inside his head? He remembered Dad's words. Had Stanley's imagination twisted reality into fiction?

Pulling his hands away from his face, Stanley looked up. Every molecule in his body froze. The stuffed fox was lying on the table in front of him. Its face was no longer resting on its front paws. Instead, its head was raised, a pair of glowing yellow eyes fixed on him.

They blinked.

And everything went black.

Chapter Ten

Tails of the Unexpected

'Watch his head, Will.' Mum's voice sounded far away. 'Scarlett, grab that blanket.'

Stanley felt Dad's solid arms around him, carrying him through the air. Holding Stanley close to his chest, Dad's heart was thumping.

'Lay him down on the sofa,' said Mum. 'It's okay, Will.'

Stanley opened his eyes to see a tangled and glistening beard. 'Dad, were you *crying?*' He couldn't hold back a grin. 'What will your mates down the pub say?'

Lowering Stanley onto the sofa, Dad sighed and shook his

head. 'Likely story,' he said with a cough, wiping his nose on the sleeve of his jumper. 'Feeling better, are we?'

Stanley watched the three frightened faces staring down at him. He wasn't sure how he was feeling.

'What happened, love?' Mum said. She reached out and stroked his hair. 'We heard a crash and found you lying on the floor.'

Stanley was suddenly aware of a throbbing pain in the back of his head. He winced, his hand reaching up to find a lump there. Searching his memory for the last thing he could remember, all he found was a bright flash of yellow. 'I... I don't know...'

Mum turned to Dad, who was nibbling his beard. 'I think we need to, er...' She gestured towards the living room door.

Dad nodded.

As soon as they had left the room, Scarlett knelt down in front of him. 'Has this got anything to do with those *voices*,' she said in a hoarse whisper, lifting his head to place a cushion under it.

'What voices?'

'The voices you heard in the walls!'

What was she talking about? Stanley searched Scarlett's face for clues. Her expression was serious, not like she was winding him up. 'You don't remember running around, shouting about people inside the walls?' she asked, nervously.

Stanley almost laughed at this, but something stopped him. The uneasy feeling in his stomach was back. He could remember feeling scared, more scared than he'd ever felt in his life, but what had he been scared of? The idea of voices was familiar, but somehow he knew that wasn't what had made him faint.

'I'm really sorry, Stanley,' Scarlett went on. 'You seemed so certain, but I just left you in there, alone, and the next minute you'd fainted.' Her eyes filled with tears. 'I know I shouldn't give you such a hard time. It's just... sometimes it feels like you want all the attention. But I guess... you really *believe...*'

Stanley didn't like the way she was looking at him, like she was measuring him for a straight jacket.

'Okay, I've spoken to the doctor,' Mum said, coming back into the room and sitting on the sofa with Stanley. 'She'll be here after her surgery finishes.'

Stanley gulped, a giant fist squeezing his lungs. 'What kind of *doctor?*'

Mum smiled. 'Just the local GP.' She pulled his legs onto her lap. 'You bumped your head pretty hard and you don't remember what happened; we just need to make sure you haven't got a concussion.'

Stanley felt his breathing return to normal. For a brief terrifying moment he'd thought they were going to pack him off to the brain hospital. But wait a minute, what would happen if Scarlett told them about the voices? What if something else made him faint? What if his memory never came back? Then would they call in *that* kind of doctor? The questions buzzed around his head like wasps in a jam jar.

Closing his eyes, Stanley fought to pull himself together. I'm *not* mad, he told himself. I'm *not mad.* Breathing deeply, he allowed the words to print into his brain; forcing them deeper with each new repetition of the thought, until the certainty grew inside his gut. Something *real* had made him faint, something very real and very dangerous, and it was time to trust himself. He would get to the bottom of whatever was going on in this house and prove to his family that he wasn't going crazy.

'Check this out!'

Stanley opened his eyes. Dad was standing in the doorway, the grin on his face almost as big as the heap of rope and canvas spilling out of his arms.

'Oh, Willard, you didn't bring that mouldy old tent,' Mum exclaimed. 'It's got more holes than your socks, and that's saying something.'

'Hey,' Dad replied, with pretend outrage. 'It's a bit *lived-in,* that's all. Just needs airing. Like my socks,' he smirked. 'There are some great walking trails around here. All we need is fresh air and a good hike to blow the cobwebs away. Don't you think so, son? I bet you're ready to get out of here for a few days?'

A surge of gratitude rushed through Stanley; and a few hours ago he would've given anything to leave this place, to pack up his rucksack and not look back; but running away wasn't the answer, he knew that now.

'It's a really great idea, Dad, but I'm still feeling dizzy,' he said in a feeble voice. 'Can we go next week instead?'

'The doctor said he'll probably need to rest for a few days,' Mum agreed.

Scarlett threw him a sideways glance. 'Yeah, I think he needs looking after,' she said, that concerned expression still fixed in place.'

'Right oh,' Dad said brightly. 'That'll give me time to patch this old thing up.' And he bounded out of the room, dragging the tent behind him.

*

Blinking eyes. Blinking yellow eyes, a voice screamed in Stanley's head.

The dark living room spun in his vision, and as wakefulness washed over him, he knew that what he'd just remembered was no dream. It had really happened. *That's what made you faint,* the voice cried now; *that fox's blinking, yellow eyes!*

A loud, rumbling snore brought him back to now. Dad was asleep in an armchair, covered from beard to slippers in a blanket. They were alone down here and, Stanley guessed, had fallen asleep in front of the telly; Mum settling them in for the night.

Blood rushed in Stanley's ears. He could hardly believe it, yet he knew it was true; the fox was *alive.* The way it had looked at him, like it was studying him, taunting him even; ordinary animals just didn't do things like that.

He scanned the room. Everything was dark and still. Could the fox be in here with them now?

Something creaked nearby.

Very slowly, Stanley turned his head – he was sure the living room door had been closed a moment ago. He tried to sit up, but it felt like an elephant was stretched out on his chest.

Staring over at Dad, there was nothing Stanley wanted more than to wake him up, to ask for his help, but he knew he couldn't, not this time. Stanley had always looked to others; always had someone to protect him, or even to laugh at his ideas until he lost belief in them, but here, in this house, it was all up to him. For whatever reason, he had been singled out to solve the mysteries of Marble Manor, and that's exactly what he was going to do. Whatever the answers were, they couldn't be as bad as the terror of not knowing; of imagining the most frightening possibilities. Perseus hadn't run from Medusa, or Theseus from the Minotaur, and there was no way he was going to run from a fox.

A strange whispering broke his thoughts; followed by a judder and a click. Then, the sound of a door opening. It had all come from across the room.

Fear and excitement bubbling in his chest, Stanley pulled himself upright, reaching for the lamp behind the sofa. Its weak bulb bathed the room in a bluish light, making it hard to tell the difference between object and shadow. His eyes landed on the door with the scorpion handle. It was half open and something had just disappeared into the dark space behind it.

A small, bushy something, its white tip shining in the lamplight.

A fox's tail.

Chapter Eleven

The Collector of Curious Secrets

The door was falling slowly back into place. Stanley flew across the living room, grabbing the scorpion handle, just as the door was about to close. Heart pounding, he slipped in through the small open space.

What was left of the living room's pale lamplight revealed a narrow passage that snaked into a distant and looming blackness. Still holding the door ajar, Stanley reached for a handle on the inside, but there was only smooth wood. Reluctantly he bent down and took off one of his slippers, using it to wedge the door open. He couldn't let it close and risk being trapped in here forever.

Even with the door propped open, Stanley knew it wouldn't be long until the tunnel twisted away from the light. He thought about using his phone torch but he hadn't bothered to charge it, given his phone didn't work here. Instead he gritted his teeth, holding an image of the creature in his mind. 'If you're not afraid of the dark,' he murmured aloud, 'then nor am I.' And with a deep steadying breath, he stepped into the darkness.

The tunnel spiralled upwards through numerous twists and turns, the stone floor cold and dusty beneath his bare foot. The thick black air seemed to be pressing down on him, as though trying to halt him in its shadowy embrace, yet somehow his legs kept walking, one hand sliding along the rough wall as a guide.

Rounding yet another corner, there appeared a faint beam of light on the ground up ahead. As he got closer, Stanley realised it was coming from beneath a closed door. Trying to ignore the clawing fear scratching at his skin, he pressed his ear against the door, hearing only his jagged breathing. Very slowly, he reached down and turned the handle. Almost to his surprise, it creaked open and he found himself inside a cluttered circular attic.

This must be one of Marble Manor's turrets, he realised, seeing too that its circular walls were lit with lamps like the ones in the priest hole. Crowds of moths danced around the lamps' orange glow, creating a strange movement of light and shadow that made it seem as though the walls were breathing. That wasn't all; creeping around the doorframe and a tiny arched window were clumps of a strange, vine-like plant. Stanley shivered, the plant looked like the bent fingers of severed hands; hands that might clasp the door shut and never let him open it again.

And it wasn't only these creeping twigs that made Stanley's heartbeat dance. Gazing around the room, it was clear that someone was living up here, or they had been until very recently.

An unmade camp bed sat at the far side of the room, a pair of woolly socks and some crumpled pyjamas sticking out from under the pillow, an open book lying on top of it. Piles of books were stacked up around the bed, bundles of wool and tweed spilling out from beneath it. On a bedside table lay a battered watch on a chain.

The fox was nowhere to be seen.

'I know you're in here.' Stanley's quivering voice was strangely loud in the silent room. 'So you may as well come out.'

Nothing. Not a single sound or movement disturbed the strange stillness.

An unwashed dinner plate lay forgotten on the windowsill. Nearby, a camping stove was perched on a chest of drawers, a few cans of food on the shelf above it. There was only one plate, one knife, one fork; one mug, one spoon. Loneliness crept under Stanley's skin.

'Ouch!' A sharp pain had stung his bare foot. Lifting it up he found a small piece of splintered glass sticking out of his skin. Wincing, he pulled the glass free, his eyes searching the carpet. All they found was a thin length of metal sticking out from underneath an armchair by the window.

Hopping over to the armchair, Stanley crouched down and pulled at the piece of metal. It belonged to a pair of battered, old-fashioned spectacles. A picture of someone elderly formed, in Stanley's mind, and that someone soon had a face... 'Archibald Marble!' he exclaimed, remembering the portrait in the living room. But why would Archibald Marble be living up here when he had a huge house? Except – this room looked more like a hideout. Stanley turned the spectacles over in his hands, seeing with a jolt that the glass of one lens was shattered. Had something happened to the old man up here? Something bad? Is that what had made the old man ill?

Stanley fell into the armchair, his mind racing with sudden images of poor old Archibald Marble trying to hide from this fiendish fox. He shifted uncomfortably; something hard was poking his thigh through the armchair cushion. Jumping up, he ran the palm of his hand over the cushion, feeling the edges of a large square object inside it. With trembling fingers, he opened the zip, pulling out a cloth bag tied up with string. The bag was new, but what was inside definitely wasn't.

It was a book, thick and heavy, the material of its dark red cover smooth as skin, with long vein-like bumps trailing over it. The words on the cover were too faded to read, but he could just make out a drawing of a black lizard surrounded by flames in a bottom corner. The name *Marble* had been woven amongst the flames in golden thread.

Lowering himself back into the armchair, Stanley lifted the book's cover. With the pages spread it was big enough to fill his entire lap and a cloud of red dust flew out. The dust hung in the air around his face and, breathing it in, a feeling of strength and pure pleasure flowed through him; the knowledge that he could do anything, be anyone, as long as he had this book.

Stanley was vaguely aware of a movement nearby, but a deep longing to read had flooded him and he couldn't look up. Engraved inside its cover was a series of symbols, twirling and swirling in such a way that he could swear they were moving. On the first page of faded parchment someone had hand written, *A Collection of Curious Secrets.* Stanley felt the corners of his mouth twitch. Secrets that would soon be his.

Something creaked behind him, but Stanley didn't care; all that mattered was this book. Its pages were packed with drawings and symbols, much of the writing was again in an unfamiliar language; but there were readable notes scribbled in the margins – *Boil lodestone in Sea Serpent skin for twenty-four hours before attempting Recludo charm... Use only Blue-bellied Scarab beetles for this protection amulet... Cow dung will replace Ox's for Dream Diviner...*

Most wondrous of all was that each page had its own smell. Many of the smells were rich and delicious; a feast of rich, succulent flavours Stanley had never before tasted. Sometimes he came across one that stung his nose and made his eyes water. One page actually made his skin crackle and he pulled quickly back from it, realising his face had been almost touching the parchment. Written across this page in bold red pen was, *Dangerous! Should only be attempted by those who fear nothing.*

Another warning on a page where a foul odour shot a knife-like pain through his head read, *DO NOT ATTEMPT! HIGH RISK OF DEATH!!* Turning this page over, Stanley felt instantly better, and he saw now that he'd landed on a new, added page, this time on clean white paper. The new page was written in English, and held instructions for something called a *Dragon's Breath Jinx – Protecting valuable objects from the fingers of foes.* Stanley read the list of ingredients aloud, 'Five pinches of black snail dust, eight fire beetle wings, the eye of a Salamander Grandis, the ground fang of an...*Apotamkin*' that word looked like.

Glancing up from the book, Stanley laughed out loud. The priest hole wasn't packed with crazy random objects. Everything down there had been collected for use in potions and spells. His skin tingled as the truth lapped over him. Archibald Marble wasn't a vet *or* a doctor, and this wasn't a storybook he was holding in his hands. This was a book of potions and magic. *Real* magic. Archibald Marble was a *Magician.*

But now, with each page he turned, Stanley could swear the book was heating up. Or maybe his hands were just sweaty. He wiped them on his pyjamas, holding the book open again, his fingers tracing a drawing of a long emerald green snake. He stopped – there was something else here, underneath the crumpled page. Turning it over he saw that this page was stuck to the one after it, except, there was a small opening at the top of the stuck together pages, and something had been slipped inside.

Poking his fingers into the gap, Stanley carefully removed a piece of white card. The word *Sermopotum* was written in that familiar sloping handwriting; splashes of brightly coloured liquids dotting the list of ingredients and how to mix them; but it wasn't clear what the potion was for.

'Sermopotum,' Stanley rolled the word around his mouth, as though trying to taste the language's origin. So many of the book's recipes were written in the same language. He thought for a long moment… was it *Latin?* A loud cry escaped him. Was *this* the book the Cabells were after?

Pulse racing, Stanley thought back to the mess in the priest hole, the books thrown on the floor, the flung open cabinets and shattered bottles. Had the Cabells been searching for the book down there? Like Dad said, being his niece and nephew, they would surely know all the ways in and out of Archibald's secret rooms. He shivered. Were the Cabells trying to steal their uncle's magic? Had Stanley been right about that loathsome pair all along?

And suddenly, he was overtaken by a horrible feeling: shame. Hadn't he been trying to do the very same thing? Wanting to keep the book for himself only moments ago?

'No, it's not right' Stanley said aloud, shaking himself. 'These are your secrets, Archibald Marble, not mine.' He leapt up. 'And if something bad really has happened to you, I'm going to find out what and help you!'

Stanley took one last look around the abandoned room, his eyes resting on the broken spectacles. He just hoped he wasn't too late.

Chapter Twelve

Breath of the Dragon

Stanley closed the book. Placing it carefully back inside the cloth bag, he gazed around the attic once more. The fox *must* be in here with him; the passage hadn't led anywhere except to this room. So why was the creature hiding again? Only a few hours ago, it had been happy enough to shove its beady face right into his.

A fire lit inside him, replacing his fear with boiling rage. All this fox did was creep about. 'Come on,' he yelled, jumping up. 'Let's see you. Or are you scared?'

Then a new idea struck him. The fox had never actually tried to harm him, or his family. All it did was watch and listen. There it would be, curled up somewhere nearby, its face turned towards them. Even when it had appeared on the table, right in front of Stanley, it had still just stared at him.

Was the fox a spy then? And if so, who was it spying for?

An ache in Stanley's hands told him he was gripping the book too tightly, and glancing down something clicked suddenly into place – *the Cabells* – the fox must be spying for them. It was the only thing that made sense. The fox was helping them to find this book.

Stanley could kick himself. All this time the book had been hidden safely away in this old armchair and now here he was, pulling it out for the fox to see.

'I'm leaving,' Stanley muttered into the silence, 'and I'm taking this book with me.' With it clutched under his arm, he marched towards the door. 'You can try to follow me,' he said, his jaw tightening, 'but you better believe I'm harder to scare than a lonely old man.'

Back in the dark passageway, Stanley slammed the door behind him. As it clicked shut, he leaned against the cool wood, breathing heavily. It felt good to be out of that room, with its secrets and sadness. He would get far away from here; hide the book somewhere only he could find it. Then, when the time came, he would return it to Archibald.

Stanley moved as quickly as he could through the musty darkness, listening for a click or a creak, any sound that would suggest the attic door had opened after him; but nothing disturbed the silent air except the padding of his uneven feet on dusty stone.

His mind whirling with all he'd discovered, it didn't seem long before that pale lamplight was piercing the darkness again and he could make out the texture of the tunnel's rough stone walls. And there was his slipper, still propping the door open.

With a last glance backwards, Stanley slipped into the living room, where thin rays of early morning sunshine were seeping in through gaps in the curtains. Sinking his freezing foot back inside his slipper, he allowed the door to click shut behind him.

'Bogey-faced tadpole!' a voice boomed out of the silence.

Stanley's heart skipped, but it was only Dad, chuckling to himself and apparently still sound asleep on the sofa. Grunting snores bounced around the walls again.

Stanley crept past Dad and out into the hallway. He was only halfway up the stairs when a prickly feeling on the back of his neck told him someone was behind him. He whirled around, but there was no one there.

Grasping the book closely, Stanley took the remaining stairs at a run and flew into his bedroom, shoving the door shut behind him, his breath coming quick and sharp.

'Calm down,' he said out loud. 'There's no one there.'

Fingers trembling in time with his heartbeat, Stanley dropped onto his bed and untied the bag. It couldn't hurt to have one last look before hiding it away. The book fell open on a spell entitled, *Plunderer's Peril – to scare away intruders and thieves.* There was a long list of ingredients and instructions, '*Mix a handful of soil from the grave of a soothsayer with two black hen's eggs. Boil with three (no more!) Salvia leaves. Create a paste by blending the boiled potion with enough calf dung so it can be spread onto…*'

Stanley stopped reading – calf dung. Was *that* the manure Dad had seen in the garden shed and had ended up on

Plunderer's Peril

To Scare Away Intruders And Thieves.

Let those who would creep
with hands of a thief,
So soon shall you weep,
for all turns to grief!

INGREDIENTS:

Grave soil – one large handful

Bunch of Salvia leaves

Black hen eggs (two.)

Large dollop of calf dung

The bell of a True Jellyfish

(Preserve the tentacles for.)
further spell work

At least twenty pearls of Mandrake Oil

INSTRUCTIONS

Mix a handful of soil from the grave of a soothsayer with two black hen's eggs.

- Boil with three (no more!) Salvia leaves.

Create a paste by blending the boiled potion with enough calf dung so it can be spread onto the bell of a jellyfish.

Dissolve all in Mandrake Oil, placing droplets of the complete concoction over all rooms of the house.

Scarlett's face?

There was a rhyme alongside the *Plunderers Peril* spell and Stanley read it aloud, '*For those who would creep, with hands of a thief, so soon shall you weep, for all turns to grief.*'

Stanley stared at the words for a long time, a light switching on in his brain. If it wasn't *Dad* behind the manure face pack and insect curry, was it this *Plunderer's Peril* in action? Was that weird stuff meant to scare them away?

It didn't make sense though; his family weren't intruders, or thieves for that matter. So why would the spell go off?

Something creaked nearby. If only this house wasn't so rickety.

Stanley's nostrils tingled; that sweet, clinging smell was back. He thought guiltily of the greenhouse, of how no one had watered the plants since their arrival at Marble Manor, but there wasn't time to worry about dying plants right now.

'*Oww!*' the book dropped from Stanley's hands, his fingers stinging; its cover was throbbing with heat. As the book fell, the *Sermopotum* recipe slipped out and, reaching for this instead, Stanley gave a loud gasp. At the very centre of the page was a tiny drawing of an animal with red fur and sparkling yellow eyes.

A fox.

The drawing's fur began to glow, a hole appearing at its centre. And the hole was burning wider, its edges black and curling.

A whisper, '*Stanley…*'

At the sound of his name, Stanley spun to face the door – the handle was *turning*. The spidery fingers of a thin hand emerged, clasping the edge of the slowly opening door like a pale spider.

Black smoke coiled in front of Stanley's eyes, rising up from the edges of that burning hole. The fox drawing was on fire and so was the rest of the page. Not just the page, the entire book!

A sea of dancing flames burst from its pages, spitting at everything in its path. Stanley watched in horror as glowing red tongues licked against his bed, the bedside table, then the wardrobe and the curtains; angry smoke filling his lungs.

The last thing he saw, before falling, coughing to the ground, was a swirling ball of purple fire, blazing through the air towards him. And suspended in the very centre of that fiery swirl, the yellow of its eyes shining through the purple haze, was the real fox, its long claws reaching out for him.

Chapter Thirteen

Millicent

Stanley had curled into a protective ball like a woodlouse; his eyes screwed shut, arms criss-crossed around his head. Any moment now fierce claws would tear through his skin; flames burn over it. With every muscle wound tight and his breath held, he waited. *Please, please let someone smell the smoke before it's too late.*

And waited.

The seconds lengthened and still nothing happened; no claws pierced his skin, nothing burned him, and now, he realised, smoke no longer stung his nostrils, no sound of crackling flames filled his ears.

Still he waited.

'Stanley... *Stanley*, are you all right?'

The voice in his ear was smooth as melted marshmallows. Something soft brushed his cheek.

'Stanley, it's okay...'

It took all his effort, given that his heart had forgotten to beat, but slowly he opened his eyes.

'Hello.'

'AAAAAAGH!' Clasping both hands over his mouth, Stanley stared at the creature that had just popped into view. Its small black nose was almost touching his as it peered at him, whiskers quivering.

'Phew,' it said with a giggle. 'I thought we'd lost you.'

Stanley hardly dared breath; his nerve endings were fizzing like firecrackers beneath his skin. 'Who are you?' he managed to whisper. 'Wh–what are you doing here?'

The fox smiled with glistening yellow eyes. 'My name's Millicent, and I live here, silly.'

It was unnerving to see a fox smile, let alone hear one speak, but here was this one, doing both. Very slowly, Stanley pulled himself up onto his elbows. 'H–how?' he stammered. 'I mean... you can *talk*. I... I don't mean to be rude, but how is that possible?'

'Archie gave me a potion of course,' replied Millicent. She giggled again and Stanley was reminded of the sniggering that had chilled him that very first day at Marble Manor. Now the sound of her voice wasn't frightening at all and, as he watched her, Stanley felt a calmness settle over him. The fox was friendly, kind even; not at all what he'd imagined.

'Come on, Stanley, you saw the *Book of Wonders*.'

'The... *what?*' He rubbed hard at his forehead.

'That's what Archie calls his magic book,' Millicent said, matter-of-factly, glancing across the room to where the book lay open. 'You read some of the potions for yourself.' She winked. 'What about the Sermi... Sumowotsit... Oh I can never say it right, but I know what it means – *Speech potion.*'

'Sermopotum!' Stanley sprang to his feet, a vision of that potion's page flashing in front of his eyes. The tiny drawing of the fox on fire. The real fox...

'...*flying,*' he exclaimed. 'You were flying towards me in a ball of flames!' He glanced around the room, where there was no longer any trace of the fire.

'Yes, that was fun,' Millicent smirked. 'It was the *Dragon's Breath Jinx*. I've always wanted to see it in action.' She jumped onto the bed, staring into Stanley's face, and whispered, 'Archie linked it to me, so that I'd always appear if it went off. You know, as part of the spell. I begged him to do it, thought it'd be fun. And it was.' The fox grinned even wider this time, showing two rows of perfect white teeth. 'I was *scary*, wasn't I?'

'Yeah,' replied Stanley, dropping onto the bed next to her. 'Pretty terrifying actually.'

'Oh good,' she said.

Stanley couldn't help smiling. Watching her now, it was hard to believe the terrible image he'd had of this funny little creature. Then, something else pulled the smile from his lips. 'There was a *hand*, Millicent. Someone was opening my bedroom door. They whispered my name.' He glanced at the now closed door. 'Who came in?'

Staring back at him, the fox's head tilted slightly. 'No one,

Stanley,' she replied softly. 'You were afraid, maybe you –'

'Imagined it?' Heat bloomed in his cheeks.

'Well, yes,' she said in soothing tones. 'A lot of strange things were happening.'

Stanley found himself laughing, 'You can say that again.'

'It wasn't *real* fire,' she went on. 'Just pretend flames from the Jinx. Archie would never harm anyone, not even his enemies.' Her voice lowered. 'Although he knows the spells to do it.'

Now Millicent's gaze turned sorrowful. 'I tried to reach you, to tell you the flames weren't real, but the spell was too strong and I couldn't get free of it. I had to wait for it to finish.'

But that wasn't what was bothering Stanley. 'I don't understand,' he said, confused. 'Why did this Dragon's Breath Jinx go off? I wasn't trying to *steal* the book or anything.'

For the first time Millicent's expression turned serious. 'You were reading out a spell, the Plu... Plumders...'

'*Plunderer's Peril?*' Stanley finished for her.

'Yes, that's it. If the book thinks someone who isn't of Marble blood is trying to use it, the Dragon's Breath Jinx goes off.'

'What do you mean, *thinks?*' Goosebumps were popping over Stanley's skin. 'You make it sound as though the book's alive.'

Millicent blinked back at him with an almost pitying expression. 'Well of course it's *alive*. It's magic, isn't it?'

Stanley watched her snout ruffle in concentration. 'Archie says the book is...sewn with power. A power that must be respected. A power that can be... intoxi...intoxi-cating... if you don't learn to master it.' She shrugged. 'I don't always understand what Archie says, but I remember every word.' Swelling with pride, she said. 'Archie says I have a fine memory.'

Thinking for a moment, Stanley said, 'I think he means that the book is so powerful it could start to control you, instead of you controlling it. Does that make sense?'

Millicent didn't look sure, but she nodded anyway, and was soon warming to her theme. 'Archie says bad people would use the book for bad things, but good people will learn good things from it.' She paused, before seeming to go on in the old man's voice, "*There is no harm in magical art that is not first in the hearts of evil men.*"

Stanley walked over to where the book lay on the floor. He picked it up carefully, relieved to feel it was no longer hot. 'Where did Archibald get the *Book of Wonders* from?' he asked Millicent, running his hands over its veiny cover.

'It's been in his family since forever,' she whispered. 'My Archie is a great magician; he invented the speech potion just for me.'

Something struck Stanley. 'Do you know why Archie hid the speech potion recipe, Millicent? It was inside two of the book's other pages.'

Her eyes darkened. 'To protect *me*. Archie said that if anyone ever came to the house, I mustn't let them know, you know, that I can talk. He said it was dangerous.'

'So *that's* why you've kept quiet for so long?'

Millicent's snout twitched. 'Yes. I knew I needed help, but I didn't know if I could trust you at first. Archibald had gone and then your family came. I just didn't know what was going on.'

Stanley reached out to touch her paw. 'Where is Archie, Millicent?'

She shook her head sadly. 'I don't know. He disappeared a few weeks ago and I've been searching for him ever since.'

Watching her sorrowful expression gave Stanley a deep pang of guilt. 'I'm sorry, Millicent,' he said. 'I thought you were spying on me. I thought you were plotting against Archibald with –'

'– Against my Archie? Never, I'd rather die.'

The tremble in her voice made Stanley's face burn, but Millicent swallowed back her tears and smiled. 'I wanted you to follow me, Stanley, when I went up to Archie's attic. That's why I left the doors unlocked.' Her whiskers twitched when she spoke next, excitement flooding her voice. 'Archie taught me the spell that opens doors without touching them, even the *special* ones to his secret rooms.' She began chanting strange words. The same words, Stanley realised, as those he'd heard whispered in the living room, just before the scorpion door had opened.

'You mean the priest hole and the attic?' Stanley asked.

Millicent blinked. 'You know about Archie's workshop?'

'Yes, my dad let me in through the cupboard under the stairs.'

'But how?' Millicent's eyes throbbed round and bright. 'How did he open the cupboard door without the opening spell?'

'He, er… *forced* it,' Stanley replied, staring at the white patch of fur on Millicent's chest, rather than meeting her eyes.

'I suppose it doesn't matter anyway,' she said with a loud

sigh. 'Now that Archie's gone.'

Millicent hung her head and Stanley saw a large teardrop drip onto the floor from the end of her nose. 'I waited for you in the attic,' she murmured. 'I was just about to come out and tell you everything, but then you found the book. I didn't know it was hidden in that chair. I was so shocked, I couldn't move.' She lifted her gaze to Stanley's now. 'Don't you see, Stanley, Archie would never have left the *Book of Wonders* behind. Never, ever. Not in a zillion years.' She shook her head sadly. 'He always told me how very secret the book was. He'd say, *"It must never fall into the wrong hands, Millicent. It is our solemn duty to protect it from the world, and the world from it."* He never let it out of his sight.'

Stanley gently wiped the tears from her soft snout. 'It's okay, Millicent, don't cry.'

'But it's not okay.' Her voice was shaking now. 'How can the book still be here when Archie isn't?' She watched Stanley for a long time. It was hard to tell what she was thinking until she spoke again. 'You will help me, won't you, Stanley? You'll help me find Archie?'

Stanley stared into those jewel-like eyes. He'd never been more certain of anything in his life. 'You just try and stop me.'

Chapter Fourteen
A Place Forgotten

'Have you found any clues?' Stanley asked Millicent, leaping to his feet again. '*Anything* that could help us find Archibald?'

She shook her head. 'Once I thought I picked up Archie's scent in the woods, but it disappeared under another smell, something horrible. I think some poor animal must've died out there.'

Remembering the smell he'd caught from the trees that day by the graves, Stanley nodded. 'I smelled that too.' And then he remembered something else; a fox, sniffing around the garden the night before; that was Millicent, searching for Archie!

Stanley thought for a moment. 'What about Archie's workshop,' he asked. 'Do you know what happened down there? It was a right mess, stuff all smashed up.'

Millicent's snout crumpled. 'Someone broke in, just before Archie disappeared. He said it was burgliars.'

'Burglars?' Stanley checked.

'They are people who steal things, Stanley.'

He tried not to smile, while Millicent's expression remained grave. 'It really frightened him. He'd hardly leave the attic after that. He said we'd be safest up there. He put Witches Hair around the door; to help stop bad things from entering.'

Stanley remembered that claw-like plant twisting around the attic door and had the feeling he might know what Archibald meant by *bad things*. 'Millicent, did Archibald ever talk to you about Aleister and Lyla Cabell?'

She tilted her head to the side. 'Who?'

'His niece and nephew.'

'Archie never spoke much about his family,' she replied. 'That's why he gave me the potion; he told me he was lonely and wanted a friend. A friend he could trust, he said.'

Stanley weighed this information in his mind. 'Did he tell you who he *couldn't* trust?'

'No.' Millicent's sparkling gaze dulled. 'Archie must've had a lot of secrets.' She was quiet for a long time, tears welling in her eyes again. 'The b–bad things got him, didn't they? And I didn't help him,' she whimpered. 'I'm supposed to be his friend.'

'*No,*' Stanley said quickly. 'None of this is your fault, Millicent.' He moved closer to her, speaking more gently now. 'Do you know a*nything* that could help us? Even something small might be really important.'

Millicent looked at him, nibbling her tiny black lips. 'There is *something*, but I might have to show you, it's hard to explain.'

'Great!' Stanley exclaimed, pulling on his trainers and moving towards the door. 'See, Millicent, you're helping Archie already.'

The door opened before he could reach it, Dad peering into the room. 'What are you doing with *that?*' he asked, yawning.

Millicent. Dad was staring straight at her. Glancing sideways, Stanley saw with a sigh of relief that she was curled up on the floor, unmoving, her head resting again on outstretched paws.

'Er...' Stanley thought fast. 'I've never seen a stuffed animal up close. I thought it was pretty... *cool.*'

'If you say so, sunshine,' Dad chuckled. 'Just checking you're all right? I woke up and you were gone.'

'Yeah, sorry about that, but I feel fine this morning.'

'That's good.' Dad rubbed his eyes. 'It's still pretty early though. Think I'll go back to bed. None of that *drums in space* music, okay?'

'No problem,' Stanley smirked, as Dad closed the door behind him.

They waited a few minutes before Stanley pulled it open again. He peered out, glancing up and down the landing. It was quiet and empty. The only sound was the pendulum tick of a large grandfather clock at the top of the stairs. The clock told him it was just after six o'clock in the morning.

'No one'll be up for ages,' he whispered to Millicent. 'Let's go.'

She trotted ahead, Stanley following her bushy tail down the stairs and into the dining room. With a sudden thrill, he watched her whisper the spell to open a hidden panel in the wall there.

'Another secret passageway?' Stanley marvelled. 'How many of them does Marble Manor have?'

'I don't know,' Millicent replied. 'I used to think there were only two.'

'Through the scorpion door and the cupboard under the stairs?'

She nodded. 'I discovered this one a few days ago. The panel was open a tiny bit, like someone had been in the passageway before me.' She fixed Stanley with a frightened stare. 'But it wasn't Archie.' Offering Stanley her tail, she said, 'Go on, grab it, and I'll show you what I found.'

With growing excitement, and thinking how silly he'd been to be so afraid of Millicent last time he'd entered a passageway, Stanley allowed her to lead him along the chill, dusty tunnel. 'I've got whiskers on my legs that help me find my way in the dark,' she called back proudly.

In no time at all, they had emerged into a very long, high-ceilinged room. It was empty of furniture except for an old grand piano and a few chairs standing against the gold-patterned wallpaper. Heavy velvet curtains covered the windows, the room lit instead by a familiar orange glow. Millicent grinned at Stanley's expression.

'The lamp wicks are soaked in a flame potion,' she said. 'They will burn for a hundred years. All the lamps at Marble Manor are the same. Archie said his great-grandmother did it.'

'This must be part of the east wing,' Stanley gasped, his eyes wandering over the silent room.

An ornate clock, no longer ticking, sat above a huge empty fireplace. Two rows of candles had melted into their silver holders, spindly cobwebs drooping between them. The walls were lined with life-size paintings, all showing dancers in bright billowing clothes.

Even with the lamps burning, the air in here was stale, everything covered in a thick layer of dust. A dead insect landed on the wooden floor in front of them and Stanley looked up to see a chandelier stretching over most of the ceiling. The chandelier's dull glasswork dripped with bedraggled spider webs and the dried-up bodies of creatures who had given up their struggle for life long ago. This felt like a place forgotten; no longer part of a home.

'I've been back here a few times,' Millicent said, gazing around. 'It's really strange.' She looked up into Stanley's face. 'This room keeps changing.'

Stanley opened his mouth to speak but closed it again, confused.

'It's true,' said Millicent. 'Every time I come in, it looks different. I just can't put my paw on it.'

Sunshine was now pouring through gaps in the curtains, its bright light glinting on the gold picture frames and illuminating clouds of dancing dust. Stanley looked again at the thick blanket of grey covering every surface. This time, he saw something new. There were paler patches on the shelves, and shadows on the walls where picture frames once hung.

Crossing the room to the back wall, he ran his hand over clean, frame-sized gaps between the paintings, some of the gaps shinier than others.

'Someone's been taking these paintings down, one by one,' he said, thoughtfully. 'It's the same on the shelves, *look!* There's round gaps in the dust between the candleholders.'

Millicent squealed. 'The floor, Stanley! There's streaks in the dust there too.'

Stanley followed these gleaming lines from the centre of the room to a set of double doors on the far side. 'Something's been dragged out,' he said, and then gave a loud gasp. '*That's* why the room always looks different, Millicent; it's being *emptied!*' The doors were held fast by a chain and padlock. 'What's through here, Millicent?' he asked, rattling the door handles.

She moved to stand beside him. 'I don't know, the unlocking spell wouldn't work on those metal things.'

Stanley shook the chain but the padlock didn't budge; unlike the door the lock looked brand new.

Millicent's face crumpled. 'But who could be taking things from in here? No one even knows about this room except Archie; and us,' she said.

'*Someone* knows,' Stanley replied. His heartbeat sped up as he thought of everything he'd seen and heard since arriving at Marble Manor - the conclusions he'd made about Millicent; how he'd got it so wrong about her. Then again, there were other things, other people, he was certain he'd got it right about.

'Come over here a minute, Millicent,' he said, walking to

the row of chairs and sitting down. 'We need to talk about the Cabells.'

When she'd joined him, Stanley took a deep breath and told her everything he could about Archibald's niece and nephew. From their odd behaviour and claims that they were renting Marble Manor out for their uncle, to Stanley's deep fear that they were trying to steal the *Book of Wonders*.

Millicent didn't interrupt once; only listened with her eyes stretched wide and her mouth half open. Even after Stanley had finished, she didn't speak for some time. When she finally did, her eyes flashed angrily. 'My Archie *ill!* It can't be true, Stanley, he's got a potion for everything. Why would he need to go to hospital in... Sweesland?'

Stanley didn't correct her.

'And letting strangers live *here?*' she went on, her claws now piercing the chair's velvet seat. 'He would never do that. Not while he still had –' She stopped, an expression of horror creeping over her face.

'– breath in his body,' Stanley finished for her, a shiver passing through him.

Millicent closed her eyes and sobbed.

Chapter Fifteen

Bad Spells
and
Worse Smells

'Oh there you are.' Mum nearly collided with Stanley when he stepped back into the dining room. 'Where did you come from, I was just in here?'

'I –'

'Still got your little friend then,' she said with a grin, nodding towards Millicent. The fox was now curled up in Stanley's arms. She hadn't been able to stop crying earlier, and he'd picked her up in the passageway, trying his best to comfort her.

Just then the doorbell clanged.

'I think it's the Cabells,' Scarlett hollered from the hallway.

Dad appeared, handing Mum a cup of tea. 'I'm not spending my Sunday morning entertaining those two buffoons!' he cried, slopping his own tea everywhere while gesturing towards the front door. 'Don't answer it, Cornelia, I mean it.'

But it was too late; it seemed Scarlett had already done the dreaded deed. With a resigned sigh to Stanley, Mum left the room, Dad sneaking off in the opposite direction.

'Oh my word, darling, you look fabulous.' Aleister Cabell's voice gushed towards them from the hallway.

'Er, this is my dressing gown.' They heard Mum reply.

Stanley lifted Millicent higher, wiping a tear from her soft face. 'This is our chance to help Archie,' he whispered. 'Maybe you'll recognise the Cabells. Maybe something in your memory will click into place.

She gave a tiny nod, her eyes still wet with tears, but with a new light shining in them.

'Ah, the young Master,' Aleister exclaimed, when Stanley joined them. 'How splendid.'

Today, Aleister Cabell was squeezed into a pair of skin-coloured jodhpurs that made the flesh of his short podgy legs and roly-poly bottom look like lumpy rice pudding. He was even carrying a riding crop and Stanley winced as he imagined this colossal man sprawled across the back of a horse, the legs of the poor beast buckling under the weight of its ginormous rider. Aleister was fatter than ever, his skin pale and sweaty. Stanley just hoped he wouldn't be expected to shake his hand again.

'And what do you have there?' asked Lyla, pointing a red-taloned finger at Millicent.

'Oh,' Stanley said, with a flick of his eyebrow. 'This fox was in Archibald's *room*. He must've liked having her around.'

Placing Millicent on a small table so that she faced into the room, he went on, 'I thought you'd know that, being so *close* to him.'

Lyla's slender body folded slightly and she dropped onto the sofa like a falling teardrop. Stanley noticed how tightly her milk white skin was stretched across her cheekbones today. Had Aleister been eating her meals for her, he wondered?

'My sister and I find it somewhat difficult keeping track of all our uncle's favoured belongings,' Aleister said, adjusting his stomach. There was a sharp note to his voice. 'He has so many.'

'That's right,' Lyla joined, ignoring Stanley now and turning her attention on Scarlett instead. 'And what has you so engrossed over there, young lady?' she asked softly.

Scarlett looked up from the armchair she was curled up on, two books lying open in her lap. 'Chemistry homework,' she grimaced. 'My worst subject.'

'Surely not,' cried Aleister, dancing across the room to join her. 'It was always my absolute *favourite*. The rainbow of chemicals; their glistening beauty and sensuous vapours. Ah, yes, the siren call of the blessed brews. How could one fail to be enraptured?'

'Er, we're just doing Universal Indicators and the PH scales at the moment,' said Scarlett.

Aleister leaned closer to her, his words just loud enough for Stanley to hear. 'Our uncle taught us many things in the wondrous art of... *Science*,' he said. 'We can show you things, dear girl. Things you've never dreamed of.'

'What was that, Mr Cabell?' Mum asked.

'Oh nothing, dear lady, just offering to help your delightful daughter with her homework.' He gave Mum a simpering smile. 'You must be exceptionally proud of your children.' His gaze darted from Scarlett to Stanley and back again. 'Two perfect children, both at the start of that wondrous journey called life. Everything ahead of them, the heights they are destined to achieve. So magical to have –'

Lyla gave a tiny cough.

'Sorry, I do tend to ramble,' Aleister apologised, shaking himself. 'But anyway, the offer is always there.'

'Actually,' said Scarlett. 'Do you know anything about –'

'*What* can we do for you both today?' Dad had walked into the room. 'We said we'd call if we found that book of yours.'

'And we're so very sorry to disturb you,' purred Lyla, getting up from the sofa and gliding towards Dad. 'It's just that we've had a letter, you see, from Uncle Archie. He's very keen that we find his book.' She smiled with her pale pink lips parted slightly.

'Do you have the letter with you?' Stanley asked, making no effort to stop the accusation ringing through his voice.

Aleister flinched, as though Stanley's words had picked at a hidden scab. 'Well *no*, it's at home,' he said quickly. Lyla meanwhile, was watching Stanley with the gaze of a hungry python; he noticed how today her eyes looked clear blue and icy, like two frozen pools.

Stanley was dying to say what he really thought about the Cabells, but instead he forced his face into a smile and said something he hoped would force them into revealing at least some of what they were up to.

'You know, I found some pages of an old book yesterday,' he said. 'They had all these weird symbols and recipes on them.' He stopped to watch the effect his words were having on Aleister and Lyla. Both their faces held a twitching expression that seemed to play out an internal struggle.

'You'll probably laugh,' Stanley went on. 'I know it sounds crazy, but I thought they were... well, they *looked...* like magic potions and spells. One even said it had a *high risk of death!*'

'Okay, that's enough!' Mum's cheeks were flushed. 'Our son has a very active imagination, and he's not been well. I'm going to have to ask you to both leave now, Stanley needs his rest.'

It was swift and unmistakable, Aleister's expression morphed into one of deep concern. He raced to stand beside Stanley, asking with a quavering voice. 'What happened, dear child? Are you better now?'

'I just bumped my head, it's no big deal.' Stanley hardly knew what to make of this change in Aleister, he seemed genuinely worried about him.

'And you've *fully* recovered?' Aleister asked now. 'The bump left no scars, I hope?' He reached out to touch Stanley's forehead, but seemed to think better of it and pulled back. Stanley was sure he'd seen a slight shake in Aleister's hand again.

Lyla moved to where Scarlett was sitting, and she did reach out to stroke the girl's cheek with a long white finger. Stanley shuddered; Lyla's finger looked like a crooked white bone against Scarlett's soft brown skin. 'Such a terrible shame it would be to blemish these perfect young faces,' Lyla said. 'Yet untouched by the ravages of life.'

Stanley watched Scarlett's nose ruffle at the woman's touch

and she pulled back. Lyla let her hand drop.

'Potions and spells, eh!' said Dad. 'I'd like to take a look at those myself!' He laughed, leaping towards Stanley and, as often happened when Dad became suddenly excited, something thunderous exploded from his backside.

Stanley heard a small squeak from Millicent as the evil vapour seeped its way around the room.

Lyla let out a strangled cry, clasping her hands over her nose and mouth. Her pale skin was whiter than ever, her eyes rolling back in her head. She staggered forwards.

'Sorry about that,' said Dad. 'I seem to have emitted a stench more potent than a tramp's underpants.'

'Will!' Mum exclaimed, rushing over to Lyla and helping her to the sofa.

In the same moment, Aleister ran to join them, and Stanley marvelled at how agile he was for such a fat man.

'My sister is rather sensitive to unpleasant odours,' Aleister said, kneeling in front of Lyla and calling her name until she was able to focus her eyes on him.

That was rich, Stanley thought, given the constant state of Lyla's perfume. It was sweeter today, but somehow more pungent. In fact it was so strong, Aleister smelled of it too.

'I'm okay,' Lyla murmured, when Aleister reached out to hold her face with two trembling hands. He looked back at Stanley with a strange smile. 'You say you found some... *unusual* pages yesterday. Tell us more.'

Scarlett gave a nervous laugh. 'You don't think these spells are... *real*, do you?'

Aleister's reply was tight in his throat. 'Oh, no, indeed not. They'll just be Uncle's eccentric doodles, but –'

'They must remain in the family,' Lyla interrupted. Her voice was weak but defiant. 'Where did you find them, Stanley, and where are they now?'

'I think they were inside an old newspaper,' he replied. 'I'm not sure where I've put them now though.'

The expressions of both Cabells collapsed. They looked gaunt and frail, like two lost ghosts, Stanley thought. He was now more convinced than ever that it was Archibald's *Book of Wonders* they were after and that whatever they wanted it for couldn't be good. Somehow he could feel their dark motives filling the air around them, building into an almost visible rain cloud. It hung there now, grey and heavy, threatening to burst over them all at any moment.

Aleister recovered first, his eyes slipping past Stanley to the living room door. He laughed suddenly, 'Yes, well, we'll leave you to your potions then, aha-ha-haaaa.' Blinking at Mum, he said, 'Although I must trouble you for the use of the lavatory first. Don't worry, I know where the nearest one is,' he chuckled, skipping out of the room.

For the first time Stanley remembered Millicent. He glanced across to where she was sitting. Her tiny nostrils were flared; her lips pulled back to reveal black gums. Thankfully no one else was looking in her direction.

Twenty minutes later, when Aleister had finally reappeared and the front door was closed behind both Cabells, Stanley climbed back up to his room with Millicent.

'Well?' he said. 'Who are they? Are they really Archibald's niece and nephew?'

Millicent stared at him for a long time before speaking. 'I don't know,' she said. 'I don't know who they are.'

'What, you've never seen them before?'

'No. Never.' She hesitated for a moment. 'But I can tell you one thing, Stanley, and that is, I've *smelled* them.' She stared at him without blinking. 'It's the worst smell there is. The sweet and sickly scent of *death*.'

Chapter Sixteen

The Strange Behaviour of Scarlett Crankshaw

It was a warm bright day and Stanley was enjoying sitting on the sweet-smelling grass of the front lawn under a cloudless peacock blue sky.

'Be sure to get my beard in all its glory, Nelly.'

Mum peered over the top of the canvas she was painting. 'If you don't stop talking,' she said, shaking her paintbrush at Dad. 'I'll give you pink sideburns and a twirly moustache to match.'

'That'd really suit you, Dad,' Stanley smirked, grabbing another sandwich from the picnic basket. It was harder to feel fearful outside the whispering walls of Marble Manor, the warm sun on his skin.

He looked across at Scarlett who was reading something

on a piece of paper. Nudging her with his foot he said, 'Look's like Mum's got her art mojo back.'

Scarlett didn't look up. Instead she carried on reading, her eyes glittering like two tiny stars.

'What's that?' Stanley asked, louder this time.

'What?' Scarlett shot him a nervous glance before staring down at the paper again. 'Oh, it's just a letter from... Bea. She's been... doing loads of cool stuff.' Scarlett jumped up. 'I might call her from the house phone actually, writing letters takes too long.' She gave a high-pitched laugh. 'Still can't believe there's no Wi-Fi here.'

'I hope Bea isn't on holiday in Spain again,' said Dad, ventriloquist style from the corner of his mouth. 'I can't see those Cabells paying our phone bill for us.'

Scarlett might've had her back to them as she'd run towards the house, but Stanley had seen her cheeks before she'd turned away. They were tinged with pink.

'D'you mind if I go in, too?' he said. 'I've got some homework to finish.'

'Blimey,' chuckled Dad, not bothering to keep his face still this time. 'Have you heard this, Cornelia? Our son is only *volunteering* to do his homework. Alert the presses! This is front page stuff!'

'Go on in, Stanley,' Mum said, chuckling. 'Anything to keep your dad's hairy trap shut.'

'A travesty,' Stanley heard Dad shout, as he made his way slowly towards the house.

Once inside, Stanley headed for the greenhouse. He was still trying to wrap his thoughts around what Millicent had told him yesterday. Could living people really smell like death? All Stanley could hope was that she was confused. Lyla definitely needed to change her perfume, but there were other smells, insistent and sickly, drifting through the rooms of this house even when the Cabells weren't around. The smells must be coming from the greenhouse, he reasoned; no one had remembered to water in there and the plants must be dying. Then again, didn't foxes live by their sense of smell?

When Stanley stepped into the greenhouse five minutes later, he was quickly covered in a fine wet spray. Shaking the water from his eyes, he breathed in the clean fresh air. The plants still grew thick and tall, their flowers fragrant and blooming, and with leaves in every shade of green. Droplets of water clung to each leaf and petal, the room, bright and colourful, reflected in their sparkling light. This was not a place of death and decay, but one of life and health.

Stanley heard a small sigh and looked down to find Millicent sitting on the floor next to him. 'Archie's most favouritest room in the house,' she said, licking a large droplet of water from the end of her nose.

'But how is this happening?' Stanley asked. 'Who's doing it?'

'Who do you think?' she grinned in reply.

'Is it a spell?'

Millicent shrugged. 'All I know is it rains from up there.' She nodded her snout at the greenhouse roof. 'Every day.'

And now that he looked closely, Stanley could see rows of small metal circles sticking out of the ceiling's iron frame, the water spraying out from them.

'It's a sprinkler system,' he said, wiping his eyes again. 'It must be on a timer.'

'Archie told me these plants come from all over the world,' said Millicent. 'He grows them for his potions.'

At that moment the water stopped and a warm mist hovered in the air. Stanley stared around them, his throat tight. 'There are no dead plants in here, Millicent.'

'I told you,' she said. 'Archie would never let them die. He loves them too much.'

A thick soup of gloom was cooking in Stanley's stomach. If the rotten smells in this house weren't coming from the greenhouse, could they really be coming from the Cabells instead? Was the stench somehow oozing out of their skin? But if that really was the horrible truth, what exactly did it mean, and why could he smell them even when the Cabells weren't in the house?

Stanley sucked in a long shuddering breath and glanced outside. Scarlett was skipping down the driveway.

'*Scarlett!*' he yelled, leaping towards the windows and banging on the glass.

She only looked briefly around before hurrying on.

He banged again, louder this time, but she'd turned into the hedge-lined lane and out of sight. 'Where's she going?' Stanley turned to Millicent. 'She *never* goes out on her own.'

*

'But where were you, *really?*' Stanley demanded. He'd cornered Scarlett in the kitchen after dinner.

'I told you,' she sighed, 'I went to the stables. They said they'd give me a free lesson if I helped muck out the horses.'

'And Mum let you go to the farm on your own?'

Scarlett stared back at him. 'Yes, Stanley, we're not in London now. It's only down the lane and she said it was okay, as long as I called her when I got there.' Her eyes flicked sideways for a second. 'Why do you care anyway?'

Stanley couldn't shake the feeling that Scarlett was lying. 'So you mucked out the horses in *those?*' he pressed, pointing down at her gleaming white trainers.

'They… lent me some boots.' Scarlett's tone was prickly. 'What's the big deal; you're acting like I was out robbing a bank.'

Perhaps Scarlett wasn't lying, or maybe she didn't like how close he was coming to the truth. Either way she switched the conversation back to Stanley. 'If I could help you, you know, to stop being so scared all the time, I would. You know that, right?'

'What d'you mean?' he said, taken aback.

'I'm just saying, if you were a bit more… *adventurous,* you might be surprised at – at how much better things turned out.' There was something in her voice that Stanley had never heard before. She didn't sound like Scarlett at all.

'I *am* adventurous, thank you very much,' he said. 'There's things I've done, things you don't know about.'

With a tiny smile she said, 'What *things?*'

For a moment Stanley thought about telling her everything. But however much her smug expression tempted him, he fought the urge. Where would he even begin? No, the truth couldn't be shared until he knew exactly what that truth was, not if he wanted her to believe him. 'It doesn't matter,' he murmured.

'I'm sorry,' she said, more gently now. 'It's just, we're stuck here for the whole summer and I think we'd have more of a laugh if you were... well, you know... a bit more chilled out.'

Stanley could feel his jaw clenching, but somehow he managed a smile. 'I know,' he said. 'I'll try, okay?'

Excitement bloomed over Scarlett's face. 'Soon,' she said. 'We'll do something adventurous soon. I'm just waiting for...' She stopped.

'For what?'

'...Nothing.' Her eyes flashed a grin. 'Leave it to me. I'll think of something.'

Chapter Seventeen

Voices In the Dark

As Stanley lay in bed that night, his mind replayed the conversation with Scarlett. Should he have told her at least some of what'd been going on? Was he crazy to think he could work it all out on his own? He definitely wasn't ready to introduce Mum and Dad to Millicent, not without risking being dragged back to London; and Millicent and Archie needed him too badly to let that happen. Yet somehow he imagined Scarlett might cope with the idea of a talking fox much better than their parents. As long as he was careful about how he told her.

Millicent stirred at his feet. Listening to her gentle snores, Stanley wondered how she could sleep so soundly. His mind crept up to Archibald's attic, the book now back inside the armchair cushion. It had seemed the safest place for it, given it had remained undiscovered there for so long.

The red glow of the alarm clock told him it was almost two o'clock in the morning. Even a few hours' sleep would be good. Stanley's hand shook slightly when he reached up to turn off the lamp, but Millicent's long deep breaths were comforting in the now black room and he felt himself drifting away; lulled deeper with each new breath, until he was soon floating in the warm calm of sleep.

'Boo!'

His heart stopped midbeat.

'Wakey, wakey.'

A woman's voice spoke close to his ear, her bitter breath stinging his eyes. Stanley froze where he lay; even allowing air into his lungs seemed impossible.

'The lights,' the woman hissed to someone over her shoulder.

The room lit up and Stanley felt his eyes stretch wide in his face.

'Hello, Stanley.' Lyla Cabell's thin lips slipped open to form a horrible smile that showed two rows of brown tinged teeth. Her skin and eyes were so pale she looked like a drawing from which all the ink had faded. But even worse, when she closed her mouth it was like staring into the lifeless face of a china doll.

Aleister stepped forward to join his sister. He was still as fat as his sister was thin, but there were black shadows under his eyes, his skin clammy and sallow, his once immaculate moustache gone. There was no pretence this time; Aleister wore a look of purest poison. 'So nice to see you again, Stanley.'

As both Cabells stared at him in cold silence, Stanley noticed traces of a white powder on their skin. It gave off a flowery smell, reminding him of the Talc Granny Crankshaw liked to wear. But unlike with Granny, this sweet smell was mixed with a familiar and revolting stink.

'So what shall we do with him?' Lyla said at last, her glassy eyes fixed on Stanley's.

Aleister cocked his head to one side, 'Good question, Lyla.' He fixed a strange and unsettling gaze on Stanley. 'How shall we *persuade* him to spill the beans?'

Still curled up at Stanley's feet, Millicent began to silently shiver. Thankfully, both Cabells only had eyes for Stanley. But when Aleister reached a bony hand towards Stanley's face, his relief was short lived. The skin of the man's wrists showed a watery thinness, revealing purple veins beneath. Finding his voice at last, Stanley screamed in horror.

'Quiet, boy!' Aleister smothered Stanley's mouth with a cold hand. A hand that began to twitch and shake on his face. Lyla reached out to steady her brother, and when she did, Stanley saw an odd glance pass between them. A second later Aleister pulled away, sucking in a long rattling breath.

'Enough of this,' he wheezed, coughing out foul breaths. 'We've wasted enough precious time, watching and waiting, day after day.' Slowly, Aleister recovered his breath, but his expression grew darker with each passing second. 'Reduced to hiding out in the walls of our own house like rats! Well, we'll not wait a second longer. Spill your guts, boy, or I'll spill them for you!'

Without warning, Aleister threw himself forward, dragging Stanley out of bed.

'Wh–what are you… talking about?' Stanley managed to splutter, wrenching himself free of Aleister's grasp. Millicent gave a tiny squeal of terror and for a brief moment, Aleister's gaze searched out the sound.

'What do you want?' Stanley cried louder, pulling Aleister's icy stare back to his.

'Darling Uncle's *little book of wonders,* of course.' Lyla's voice was softer than a whisper and much more dangerous. 'We know you know where it is, Stanley, and we know you know what it *does.*' All traces of beauty had vanished from her face, her voice trembling with a quiet hatred when she said, 'We *know* you were using the book yesterday, we were here, we smelt the smoke. Lucky for you, those flames saved you.'

Stanley shuddered at the memory of the spidery fingers opening his bedroom door, just as the Dragon's Breath Jinx had gone off. He should never have doubted himself; of course he'd not imagined it; who else could those bone white hands have belonged to but a Cabell.

With a quick glance at Millicent, Stanley backed slowly towards the door; if she just stayed still, he could run without them ever realising the truth about her.

'You're wrong,' he said, fighting to keep his face blank as he reached behind him for the door handle. 'I don't know what you're talk –' Panic rose like a wave in Stanley's chest. The door was locked.

'Stop. Lying!' Lyla exploded, lunging at Stanley with a fearsome scream.

But Millicent got there first. Leaping suddenly from the

bed, the squealing fox landed on Lyla's head, smothering the woman's thunder-struck face with fur and claws. 'Don't – You – *Dare* – Hurt – Stanley!'

Spinning on the spot, Lyla tried frantically to wrench herself free of Millicent, but she was clearly holding on with everything she had. 'Aleister, help me!'

But Aleister's mouth had dropped open. 'A *talking fox!* He gave a sudden roar of laughter. 'Oh, Sister, if we were ever in doubt of Uncle Archie's remarkable talents, we must doubt no more.'

At these words, Millicent glanced up at Aleister, Lyla seizing the opportunity to yank herself free. She screamed, hurling the startled animal to the floor. 'Talents he wastes on vermin like *that!* Lyla gasped, staring at Millicent and Aleister with equal amounts of fury.

The sound of bones creaking followed Aleister when he crouched down in front of Millicent, a wicked gleam in his ice blue eyes. Stanley's stomach lurched when he made to stroke Millicent's face, and she recoiled from his hand, her black snout ruffled in disgust. Aleister grinned even more horribly, and then made a grab for her neck, lifting her high into the air.

'*No!*' Stanley flew at Aleister, only managing to slam into his stomach. Stumbling backwards, Stanley clamped a hand to his cheek. He could feel a bruise rising there from the sheer density of Aleister's huge gut.

'Ouch,' Aleister said, a sarcastic smile twitching his thin lips. 'I bet that hurt.' Millicent was scratching at his fingers, gnashing her teeth, but he held her so tightly she was soon struggling to breathe and fell limp.

'That's better,' Aleister said, smiling openly now.

Lightning bolts of rage exploded inside Stanley's body, and he propelled himself at Aleister once more, this time reaching for the bony hands wrapped around Millicent.

Quick as a flash, and with a sneer of enjoyment, Lyla jumped between them; Aleister lifting Millicent higher and sighing in a bored sort of way as he dangled her out of Stanley's reach,

Glancing from Aleister to Lyla and back again, Stanley summoned every last drop of courage and yelled at the top of his voice, 'MUM! DAD! HEEELP!' He ran for the door again, his shaking fingers furiously rattling the handle.

From across the room, Lyla crowed, 'Shame you chose a bedroom so far away from the rest of your darling family, Stanley. How will they ever hear you?'

'Now, my advice,' Aleister said lazily, 'would be to tell us where the book is.' He lifted his free hand, twirling it theatrically. 'You've seen for yourself how these fingers of mine have a mind of their own. How long before they start shaking, and *tightening.*' He leered nastily at Stanley. 'Before we know it, they could have completely strangled the life out of this poor dear creature.'

Stanley watched in horror as Millicent's eyes bulged inside Aleister's twisting grip. 'Stop!' he yelled. 'Don't hurt her; I'll tell you. Just let her go!'

'No, Stanley, *don't,*' Millicent gasped, her eyelids closing now. 'I'm… I'm not worth that.'

'You are to me.' Stanley could feel hot fat tears welling in his eyes, but he shook them away. 'Let her go and I'll… I'll tell you.'

Aleister shrugged, flinging Millicent at Stanley. 'Seems a fair deal to me.'

Stanley caught her, holding her shivering body close. He stared at the Cabells, his stomach twisting at the thought of what he was about to do.

'The book is in... *the turret attic...*through the scorpion door.' He paused, the words clinging to his throat. 'In – inside Archibald's... *armchair.*'

Lyla licked her lips and a delighted quiver passed through her voice when she said, 'Thank you, Stanley. Thank you very much indeed.'

A wicked grin split Aleister's face. 'And something for you in return. A little gift from us; we know how poorly you sleep.' Reaching into his pocket, he brought out a dandelion, its fruiting head a perfect sphere of feathery seed parachutes. Except this dandelion's sphere wasn't white, it was bright blue. 'Just to prove how grateful we are.'

'Let me,' Lyla said, taking the dandelion from her brother and slithering towards Stanley with snake-like wrath.

He glanced frantically around, but there was nowhere to run, and before he knew what was happening Lyla had blown the dandelion into his face. The little blue parachutes combined with her foul breath, making him choke.

In only a few pounding heartbeats, the room began to spin, and Stanley felt his limbs tingle, then go numb. Stumbling forwards, he dropped to his knees. 'Wh–what... have you... done to me?'

'Nighty night,' Aleister crooned, pulling Millicent out of Stanley's now useless arms. 'This *creature w*ill be most helpful to us.' He narrowed those pale eyes at Stanley. 'And know this, boy; if you follow us, or get anyone else involved, you may soon get a whiff of *fox stew*.'

Cold swallowed Stanley's heart. He fought to stay conscious but dark misty clouds were closing in on him from all sides and he tipped, face down, onto the carpet. From somewhere faraway he heard Lyla's voice singing out the opening spell. With his last drop of energy, Stanley raised his head towards the sound. A blurred yet terrifying vision met his eyes – Aleister and Lyla dragging Millicent through an open panel in his bedroom wall.

The last thing Stanley saw was Lyla's head, peering back at him through the opening. 'See you soon,' it whispered.

Chapter Eighteen

The Nightmare that Wasn't

Golden light shone through Stanley's eyelids. Warmth stroked his cheeks. He couldn't quite open his eyes, but that didn't matter; he was relaxed and happy, his body floating on a soft bed of – *No, wait,* that wasn't right. He shifted slightly; something hard was pressing against his back. There was pain in his knees, his *head.*

Stanley forced his eyes open, blinking back the bright morning sunshine pouring in through the window. He was alone in his bedroom, but the Cabells' presence still lingered in the foul–smelling air around him.

Then he remembered the blue dandelion and rubbed his

nose, it still itched from where those sleep-inducing seeds had been blown in by Lyla Cabell. 'She... she *took Millicent,*' he stammered aloud.

A dull headache followed Stanley as he crawled to his feet. Stumbling across the room he traced his hands over the wall in front of him, hot fear prickling his skin. There was nothing, not even the tiniest break in the wallpaper; no clues at all, to where a section of the wall had opened up last night, swallowing the Cabells, and *Millicent,* whole.

Imagining what they might be doing to her at this very moment, Stanley's fear turned to panic. 'Bring her back!' he yelled, pummelling the wall. Panic, fear and frustration all competed for space inside his chest until he was attacking the wall with his feet as well as his fists, screaming Millicent's name.

'*Stanley,*' Mum's frightened voice was behind him. '*Stop it!*' He felt her hands grip his shoulders, pulling him round to face her. 'Wh–what happened to your face?' Her skin paled at the sight of his bruised cheek.

'Mum, listen,' he said, panting for breath, 'I know how this is going to sound, but it – it's... *the Cabells.* They came into my room last night and they –'

'The Cabells... *in your room?*' Mum's voice quavered. 'What did they want, Stanley? What did they *do?*'

The fear in Mum's eyes was unsettling, but he couldn't help feeling relieved that she believed him.

'Will!' she yelled, running to the bedroom door. 'Willard, I need you up here, now!' Turning back to Stanley, she said slowly, 'I want you tell me everything that happened, Stanley. It's okay.'

'No, Mum, it's nothing like okay.' Panic gripped him again. 'I've got to find another way in. I've got to find –'

'Hey, what's going on?'

The sight of Dad sparked an idea. '*The priest hole!*' Stanley exclaimed. Aleister and Lyla may have the book now, but there were plenty of other books down there. The door to the cupboard under the stairs was still off its hinges, so he could easily get down there. Surely it was possible that there was another of Archie's books that contained the opening spell? *Yes*, Stanley tried to weave around Dad; if he could just find the spell, he could open the wall in his room and go after the Cabells.

But Dad wouldn't let him pass.

'Let me go!' Stanley demanded.

The hurt look on Dad's face stopped Stanley in his tracks. He hesitated and, pulling in a deep breath, stared straight up into Dad's eyes. 'It's the Cabells, Dad... they've been coming in here without us knowing... sneaking into the house... watching us. They want Archibald Marble's *Book of Wonders* and they'll do anything to get it.'

Dad looked from Stanley to Mum. 'That pair of weirdos... *in this house?*' There was a dangerous edge to Dad's voice when he pointed at Stanley's cheek. 'Tell me they didn't do *that?*'

Mum nodded, her eyes wide with fear. 'He said they came in *here.*'

'Into his bedroom?' Dad shook with rage. 'How could they get in here without us seeing them?'

'Just because you don't see people,' said Stanley, 'it doesn't mean they're not there.' He gave Dad a meaningful look. 'There's more than one hidden passageway. Loads more; they are all over the house. The Cabells have been using them to spy on us since the first day we arrived. I heard them in the walls, *smelled* them; I just didn't realise...'

But Dad was only interested in one thing. 'Let me get this straight, Lyla and Aleister Cabell have been coming into this house, in secret. They were here, in your room, and they... *hurt you?*'

'Yes,' said Stanley. 'But I think they've hurt Archibald Marble much worse, and now –'

Dad was no longer listening. 'I'll knock their bloody blocks off!' he roared. 'I bet old Marble has a pistol around here somewhere...'

Mum looked scandalised but didn't argue.

'Dad!' Stanley yelled. 'You've got to listen! The Cabells have got Millicent. She's not safe!'

Dad stopped mid rant. 'Millicent? Millicent *who?*'

The memory of Lyla dragging Millicent's half conscious body across the room stomped through Stanley's memory. His breath felt sharp in his chest. 'The *stuffed fox...* she's... not really stuffed,' he blurted, 'she's *real* and she can *talk*. Archibald gave her a potion. Oh, why didn't I get her to teach me the opening spell?' Stanley was finding it hard to breathe. Pins and needles prickled in his hands and feet. 'We've got to find her,' he choked, grabbing the front of Dad's jumper. 'We've got to find her before it's too late.'

The fury melted from Dad's face, and he exchanged a look with Mum. 'What are you like, son?' he said, holding Stanley by the shoulders and shaking his head. 'You've been dreaming, that's all.'

'Goodness,' Mum joined in, 'it's lucky your dad didn't find

that pistol.'

'I wasn't dreaming!' Stanley shouted. 'This wasn't a nightmare. The Cabells have been hiding out inside the walls of this house and…' Stanley's brain whirled, '…and taking things from the east wing too, I think. Dad, you said yourself food's been going missing, and Mum, you noticed things being moved. They've been watching us, trying to see if we'd found that book, and last night, they came in through my bedroom wall, and they –' Stanley stopped, watching the incredulous look on Mum and Dad's faces.

'Through the wall?' Dad chuckled. 'What are they, *ghosts?*'

'There's a panel.' Stanley ran over to the wall, but it was no use, he didn't know how to open it, and the look of pitying disbelief in his parents' eyes was enough to silence him.

'Even secret passages have a button to press, or a lever to pull to get into them,' said Dad. 'There's nothing on that wallpaper except a dodgy pattern.' His voice softened as he smiled down at Stanley. 'It was a dream, son, nothing more. You've been asleep half the day, it's not surprising.'

'That's right,' said Mum. 'I came up here to get you up; lunch is ready. Come and have something to eat. It'll make you feel better.'

Stanley stared at his parents' relieved faces and knew it would be impossible to convince them that there were passageways weaving behind every wall in this house; and even more unbelievably, that the only way to open them was with a spell. He breathed deeply. This whole thing had started with him and he would just have to finish it. Alone.

'I guess you're right,' he said flatly, 'just my imagination again. I'll get dressed… be down in a minute.'

'Don't be long,' said Mum, before they both left the room.

Hearing their voices fade away, Stanley threw on some clothes and raced out of his bedroom, colliding with Scarlett in the hallway.

'I was just coming to find you,' she said. 'How about –'

'Not now.'

Stanley felt Scarlett's hurt chase him down the stairs, but he didn't turn back. He couldn't; he had to get to the priest hole and go through Archibald's books, his notes, anything that might reveal a way into that passageway and after the Cabells.

Before Stanley could reach the cupboard under the stairs, a movement in the living room caught his eye. He peered through the half open door. Yes, there it was again; a small shape had flashed through the far door and into the corridor leading to the greenhouse. He could've sworn...

'*Millicent...*' he called, in a hopeful whisper, racing into the greenhouse. 'Millicent are you in here?'

Only silence replied, and after many long, fruitless minutes of searching, Stanley turned to leave. Except – he couldn't shake the feeling that something wasn't right in here. His eyes scanned the long rows of pots on the ground, a sharp breath pinching his chest; one plant had a large section missing, like it had been ripped from the roots; another had what looked like teeth marks in it.

When a petal dropped through the air, landing on Stanley's shoulder, his eyes followed its path to a group of pots lying at strange angles inside their hangings. Moving closer to get a better look, he almost stepped in a pile of soil and broken pottery. A pot had fallen and smashed, the plant inside stripped of its leaves and petals. And that wasn't all; tiny footprints were scattered in the spilt earth – an animal's footprints.

'Stanley?' Scarlett's voice murmured behind him. 'Are you all right? Mum just told me about your nightmare. Something about a talking fox called Matilda?'

Turning around, Stanley saw that Scarlett was trying to hold back a grin. 'Her name's *Millicent*.'

'Er, okay.' She looked at him uncertainly, her expression hard to read. 'Well, I think I've got something that'll cheer you up, anyway.' She stared at him, a tiny light coming into her eyes. 'Are you ready for an adventure?'

When he didn't reply she seemed to take his silence for approval.

'I'm going out with Mum now, but meet me back here at midnight, okay?'

'*Midnight.* What? Why?'

'Just trust me,' she whispered. 'I'm not giving you any clues, don't want to spoil the surprise.' She turned quickly away, racing out of the greenhouse.

Chapter Nineteen

The Last Passageway

Scarlett wore the same wide-eyed look when Stanley met her in the greenhouse at midnight, and was jigging about like someone dancing barefoot on hot sand.

'At last!' she said. 'Ready?'

Stanley stared at her flushed cheeks. 'Depends where we're going?'

'If I told you that, it wouldn't be a surprise,' she replied. Grabbing his arm and pulling him along behind her, she gave him little chance to object. 'Don't look so worried, Stanley, this is going to be cool.'

Moments later they were standing outside the cupboard

under the stairs. Stanley exhaled loudly. If all this was about Archibald Marble's workshop, it was hardly breaking news.

Scarlett lifted the battered door aside and pulled a torch from her pocket.

'Scarlett, I don't mean to spoil –'

'Shhh,' she said in a loud whisper, dragging him through the doorway. 'You'll wake Mum and Dad up.'

Stanley allowed her to lead him down the passageway, even though he knew its twists and turns well enough himself, having only stepped out of the priest hole an hour ago. The whole day had been spent searching through Archibald's books and notes; he'd even got Dad to translate more of The Leechbook, but with no luck. Stanley hadn't found a single hint on how to open the secret doors and time was running out. And now here was Scarlett, wasting more of those precious minutes.

Finally, they climbed out of the fireplace, but Scarlett didn't stop here. Instead she barely looked up as she marched Stanley across the room, weaving through the narrow spaces between tables and cabinets, not slowing down for a single second.

'Almost there,' she said, yanking him harder when he tried to resist.

'Scarlett, wait!'

She whirled around. 'I *know* you've been down here before. So have I.' She frowned at the look of surprise on Stanley's face. 'Dad does show *me* stuff too, you know. Anyway, Archie's workshop isn't the surprise.' She pointed to a long section of wall covered with copper-coloured tiles. '*That* is.'

At first glance Stanley couldn't see what she was pointing

at, until – it was easy to see how he'd missed it, yet there it was, veiled amidst the painted tiles: a small, rusty door handle.

Dank air seeped out when Scarlett yanked the door open. She uttered a small gasp of surprise, but pressed on anyway, stepping swiftly through the doorway. When she turned back to face Stanley her blue eyes were shining brightly. 'Come on, you promised you'd be a bit braver, remember?'

Staring into the murky gloom Stanley felt a rush of fear and excitement. 'Has this got anything to do with… the Cabells?' he asked, trying to hide the tremble in his voice.

Laughing, Scarlett stepped into the tunnel. 'This is about you and me having an adventure,' she called back, pointing her torch into the darkness. 'Are you coming or not?'

This wasn't an answer, Stanley knew that, but if there was even the slightest chance this tunnel could lead to Millicent, he would take it; however dangerous it turned out to be. Shaking off the last terrifying image he'd had of the Cabells, Stanley followed.

Instead of twists and turns, this passageway carried them completely straight. It seemed to go on and on, its musty air filling their lungs, and making them both cough every few seconds.

Soon, Stanley noticed a different kind of smell. It wrapped itself around his tongue and clawed the back of his throat, growing more potent with each new breath he took: it was the foul and unmistakeable taste of the Cabells.

Stopping dead in his tracks, he called out, 'I'm serious, Scarlett, you have to tell me the truth about where we're going. There's things you don't know, *important* things about –' He paused, knowing how this would sound. '– the Cabells.

They're dangerous, Scarlett, and if this has anything to do with them, we need to think it through, we need to have a plan.'

'I'm not listening.' Scarlett snorted. 'You're obsessed with the Cabells and you're spoiling all the fun! Now come on, I – OWW!'

Stanley walked straight into her back.

'Looks like we're at the end of the passage,' she murmured, rubbing her knee. The torch shone over a set of stone steps leading to a hatch in the tunnel roof. 'I guess we go up.' Throwing a grin back at Stanley, she started to climb.

Screwing up his courage, Stanley followed. If Aleister and Lyla were on the other side of that hatch, he resolved, then this time he'd be ready.

'Hold this.' Scarlett handed him the torch. 'Point it up there.'

In the torchlight, Stanley watched her unclick the latch and push the hatch open with both hands. Cool air played with his hair as she climbed out. Her feet disappeared and then there was silence.

'Scarlett...?'

All he could hear was the soft whistle of wind and what sounded like the distant cry of nocturnal creatures.

'Come on,' she called suddenly. 'We're here.'

Scrambling up the ladder after her, Stanley stepped out into a forest. It must be the one surrounding Marble Manor and, judging by how far they'd travelled along that passageway, they were now deep inside it. Here, the trees grew close together and although Stanley glimpsed the glow of a full moon above, thick branches blocked out most of its light, the ground lost beneath a knotted blanket of roots.

Something rustled nearby.

'Just the wind,' Scarlett said. Although her face was masked by the inky night, Stanley still caught the uncertainty in her voice.

'What are we doing here, Scarlett?'

'It's just over –' Her words faltered. A howling cry had carried on the wind towards them.

It was impossible to see anything of the nearby craggy hills through the dark swaying branches, but hearing that long howl made the moors feel as close as the trees around them. Stanley couldn't shake the vision of the Barguest, its red eyes glowing with hell fire, skulking in the trees and ready to pounce.

'Tell me *that* was the wind, too.'

'Let's get inside,' Scarlett whispered hastily, hurrying back to Stanley and clasping his arm. He turned towards the hatch again, but she pulled him in the opposite direction. 'No, we're going over *there!*'

Stanley followed her pointing finger to a clutch of trees in the distance. The branches here were further apart, a dense dark shadow rising up between them. The shadow was big, like – 'A house?' Stanley cried. 'Who lives there?'

She didn't reply, just tiptoed forwards. As he followed her towards the small stone building, Stanley was sure Scarlett's silence betrayed the same fear that was filling his chest,

It wasn't a house, rather a tiny church. He could just make out the cross on its moss-covered spire. Its crumbling body stood lonely and abandoned amongst sprawled, clasping branches that seemed to want to drag its ancient walls down into the earth.

Scarlett shone her torch over the front of the building and Stanley noticed a stone plaque sitting just above the arched doorframe. It bore what looked like a Marble family crest: a stone shield with their name held high over the outspread wings of a burning dragon. A date read 1308.

Scarlett's fingers moved to lift the door latch.

'Wait!' Stanley hissed.

But it was too late. The door creaked open to reveal a square room, its stone walls lined with flickering candles and high narrow windows. Scarlett gasped when she saw the drooping spider webs hanging in every groove and corner, but she reached for Stanley's hand and, holding him tight, pulled him inside.

The only sign of the building's former life as a chapel was a large stone altar upon which sat a basket of speckled turquoise eggs, a stone bowl, and an ancient-looking stone tablet, rust coloured and crumbling, and etched with what looked like hieroglyphics.

What took up most of the room, what drained every drop of air from Stanley's body, was a table, clouds of colourful vapours spiralling out of the many glass bowls on top of it.

And standing at the table, a vial of red liquid held high in his trembling hand, was a very tall, very old, man. Stanley recognised the *Book of Wonders* that lay open in front of him.

Could it really be – 'Archibald Marble?' Stanley's voice cracked in disbelief.

At the sound of his name the old man looked up. Very slowly, he removed a pair of round eyeglasses, rubbing their lenses against the tweed of his waistcoat. His thin wrists looked lost inside the baggy sleeves of a grubby white shirt, the collar equally loose around his wrinkled neck. When a ghostly beam of moonlight lit his pale face through the window above, Stanley could see the deep lines of his forehead, the puffy ring under each dull amber eye.

'Ah,' he said at last, dragging a hand across his forehead. Clumps of white hair clung to his skin in wet strands. 'The young twins, I presume?' He looked sideways. 'Am I right, Millicent?'

There was something unnatural in the way he spoke, like the voice was borrowed from someone else. A chill seeped into Stanley's heart, then froze it completely; Millicent was sat at the end of the bench, a leaf dangling from between her shiny white teeth.

She nodded.

The old man ran his watery gaze over Stanley and Scarlett, and said, 'Come on in then, we've been waiting for you.' His expression was as blank as a new piece of paper.'

Stanley glanced at Scarlett through the flickering half-light. Her startled eyes were darting from Millicent to Archibald Marble and back again.

The old man swirled the vial in a shaky hand, spilling a few drops of liquid as he poured its contents into a bubbling glass bowl. 'Forgive me for not welcoming you properly,' he said, stirring the liquid now, 'but this is rather a delicate potion, and I cannot –' he paused, candlelight the only thing dancing in those glassy eyes, '– afford to make mistakes.'

Watching the potion turn from pinkish red to a swirling mass of darkest purple, Stanley called suddenly, '*Millicent,* what is that potion? What's going on? Wh- where are the

Cabells?'

'*Millicent..?*' Scarlett croaked, 'she's… she's *real*.'

Not paying attention to either of them, Millicent didn't look up at the sound of her name. Instead she continued moving busily among a pile of plants at the far end of the table, shredding leaves with her sharp little teeth before dropping them into a bowl.

'I fear this day will hold little you expected of it,' Archibald Marble said with a sigh. His gaze was back on the twins now, but it looked through them to somewhere else, somewhere far away. 'I'm afraid it cannot be helped. We do what we must, however unpleasant it tastes.'

'What does *that* mean?' Stanley said, pulling Scarlett closer. 'What are you doing here?'

'Waiting for you and your sister, of course.' Archibald blinked slowly. 'We are going to need your bodies, I'm afraid.'

Chapter Twenty

Aleister's Secret

Scarlett's hand gripped Stanley so tightly he could feel her heartbeat pulsing in her fingertips.

'Our *b–bodies?*' she stammered, staring at Stanley with big round eyes. 'Wh–what does he mean?'

Stanley leapt towards the table, Scarlett just clinging on. '*Millicent, w*hat's going on?'

She gave no reply, only catching his eye for the tiniest moment before turning back to her task of collecting and chewing the plant leaves.

'I… I don't understand.' Scarlett was trembling now. 'Archibald isn't supposed to be here. They said he'd never come back from Switzerland.'

'*Who* said?' Stanley demanded.

The pink tinge had returned to Scarlett's cheeks. 'You were right, Stanley, I *did* bring you here to meet the Cabells,' she said, her voice somewhat high-pitched. 'They left a note in my bedroom, and I met up with them. We've been in contact ever since.' She glanced around with a growing sense of panic. 'Why aren't they here?'

Stanley felt his throat tighten as Scarlett went on, barely drawing breath.

'Aleister told me Marble Manor was full of secret things that would amaze us,' she said. 'It was *them* who showed me Archie's workshop, not Dad.' Her gaze dropped for a moment. 'It feels like it's always *you* he wants to hang out with, Stanley, never me.' She looked back up at him with an almost pleading expression. 'Lyla said Archibald had taught them *real magic;* that all I had to do was bring you here and they would show us everything; share all they'd learnt with us. She kept saying how there are wondrous things all around us, if we only –'

'– know how to look,' Archibald said wistfully.

Scarlett watched the old man for a moment, before turning back to Stanley. 'We have to find the Cabells,' she said, grabbing him with both hands. 'They'll help us, I know they will.'

From her place on the table, Millicent gave a hollow laugh.

'So you've remembered your voice at last,' Stanley yelled, hardly bearing to look at her. 'How could you, Millicent? I was your friend and all this time you were tricking me, with *him!*' Stanley glared at Archibald Marble, who was now stirring the potion and quietly humming to himself.

When Millicent finally met Stanley's eyes, hers held none of their former sparkle. 'It's not that simple, Stanley.'

'Yes, it is,' he replied in a low angry voice. 'You've been doing *his* dirty work.' He jabbed a finger at Archibald. 'Helping him trap us here.' Stanley's words faltered slightly as he pulled Scarlett backwards towards the door. 'B–but you're not getting any part of our... *b-bodies,* do you hear me? This time I'm getting my parents. *This* time we'll go to the police.' They were almost at the door now. 'We'll tell them how the Cabells have been working with Archibald Marble to break into the house; how they attacked me and –'

Scarlett's mouth dropped open at this last part, but it wasn't her voice that cut Stanley off.

'And *what*, Stanley?'

He spun around. Aleister Cabell filled the tiny doorway behind him and the eyes that flashed at Stanley were as bright as lightning and a startling turquoise blue.

Moving forward as he spoke, Aleister forced the twins backwards into the chapel again. 'I suppose you'll tell the police all about how we walk through walls, and about dear Uncle's potions.' Aleister's lip curled beneath a smooth new moustache. 'Oh, and about his *talking fox,* of course.'

There came the sound of cruel laughter before Lyla appeared too. 'Yes, that all sounds perfectly plausible to me.' Stanley caught the gleam of triumph in her face before she turned to close the door.

Stanley gasped when she faced them again. Like her brother's, the once icy pools of Lyla Cabell's eyes had transformed into a deep and piercing blue.

'I must confess, Scarlett,' Aleister said now. 'I was doubtful of you getting Stanley here, what with him being such a scaredy cat and all.' Malice shone in Aleister's thin face as he went on. 'I thought we were going to have to come and get you ourselves, but here you both are.' He turned to Lyla. 'It seems you were right, sister mine. She's not *quite* as much of a fool as I thought.'

Smiling wickedly, Lyla grasped Scarlett's face in her bony fingers, forcing Scarlett to look up at her. 'Not exactly *clever* though,' she said. 'In fact, nearly as dim-witted as her father, breaking that line of salt and finally allowing us...' she laughed, '*impure ones,* to walk freely through the front door of Marble Manor.' A black eyebrow flickered. 'The door of what will soon be *our* house.' Now, Lyla moved her face so close to Scarlett's they were almost touching, her nose hovering over Scarlett's skin like she was breathing her in.

Too afraid to move, Scarlett's eyes peeled back in terror.

Every muscle in Stanley's body clenched. 'Let – Her – Go.'

'Now, now, Stanley,' Lyla said, releasing Scarlett and gliding towards him instead. 'Things can be done the easy way, or the *hard* way.' She peered down imperiously, her voice a nasty growl. 'Don't tempt me to use the latter.'

The longer he stared back at her, the more Stanley saw how different Lyla was today. Relaxed and strong, and there was no trace of the white powder on either Cabell, and – Stanley pulled in a sharp breath; there was now only the slightest trace of that repulsive smell. He'd been too angry to notice it before.

Aleister gave a loud cough. 'Well, that's the niceties over with.' Pulling a small package from his pocket, he crossed the room to join Archibald. 'Now to business.' He held up the brown-papered bundle for Archibald to see. 'Brimstone, Uncle, just as you requested. Although why you couldn't keep some in your own stores, is beyond me.' He sighed. 'But then again, you've always been weak.'

'Yes, yes, very weak,' Archibald murmured in agreement. Glancing up, the old man seemed surprised to find Aleister standing there in front of him.

When Aleister threw the package onto the table and began to unwrap it, a faint smell of rotten eggs emerged from inside.

Scarlett was breathing jaggedly, her eyes fixed on Aleister. 'Look at his hands,' she managed to whisper. 'They're not shaking anymore.'

Staring back at her, Stanley said, 'I don't think that's the most important thing here – whatever that potion is, I'm pretty sure it's for us!' He watched Scarlett's expression grow livid with fear.

Aleister had turned to Millicent now. 'You have the Wormwood from the greenhouse?'

She nodded, picking up a pale green shrub in her teeth and dropping it into the glass bowl.

'Hurry up,' Lyla hissed. 'I won't wait a second longer.'

'Be calm, sister dear,' Aleister cooed. 'The final ingredient is about to be added.' He finished unwrapping the package, pushing its contents towards Archibald. The Brimstone was a pale yellow powder.

'Come on then, Uncle.' Aleister's voice had begun to shake, but Stanley could tell it was a quiver of excitement rather than fear. '*Now* would be good.'

The room fell silent as everyone watched Archibald in grim fascination. Poking a silver spoon into the yellow powder, he added three piles to the bubbling mixture. Instantly the contents of the bowl began to steam and froth, and a long anguished scream poured out, splitting the foul air like the skin of a rotten apple.

Millicent squealed and ran to the end of the table, while Aleister and Lyla both shrieked with laughter, leaping together and clasping each other with joyous cries.

'The day has come at last!' Aleister exclaimed.

'It all starts here,' Lyla's shivering voice sung in reply.

While the Cabells stared into each other's elated faces, Stanley watched Millicent creeping back towards Archibald with something in her mouth, the old man not noticing when she dropped whatever it was into his pocket.

'The potion will be ready when the mixture lies smooth and silent,' Archibald said quietly. Stanley tried to follow the old man's gaze, but it was looking into empty space again.

Aleister whirled in their direction, no longer laughing. 'And how long will *that* take?'

'It could be an hour, it could be twelve,' Archibald replied flatly. 'How about a cup of tea?'

'Twelve hours!' Lyla almost choked on her words. 'You old fool!' She grabbed her brother, shaking him. 'It's a ploy, Aleister. He's up to something, I just know it!'

'Now you know that's not possible,' Aleister replied, his eyes wide with meaning. 'Lyla – will you – *stop it!*' He was struggling to speak now that she was shaking him so violently.

'I can't stand it,' she shrieked. 'I –' She stopped, looking down at her hands.

Stanley had to rub his eyes to be sure of what he was seeing. It was all too real; Lyla had thrust her fingernails through her brother's shirt and deep into the flesh of his fat arms.

Aleister let out a long sigh, yet showed no sign of pain. In fact, not a single drop of blood had emerged from the wounds. Everyone stared at his arms. All except Archibald, who was filling a kettle.

'Oh, what does it matter if they know,' Aleister said, wiping his forehead. 'I'm sweltering in here. You may as well finish the job, Lyla.'

The shock of what she'd done seemed to bring Lyla to her senses. Yanking her fingers out of her brother's arms, she plunging them into his chest instead. 'I don't know why we can't keep it in a bank like normal people,' she complained, tugging with all her slender might.

'I've told you before,' Aleister replied, fighting to keep his balance, 'I don't trust anyone with my cash except me.'

Lyla grunted and snorted, until, with a final effort, she ripped Aleister's enormous chest and stomach clean away. Piles of money spilled out onto the carpet, Aleister pulling at his arms and legs in the same way.

Before long a skinny Aleister Cabell was standing inside a knee-deep stack of saggy clothing and wads of sweaty bank notes.

Stanley recoiled in shock – the hideous man had never been fat: he'd been wearing some kind of cash stuffed bodysuit.

Aleister's mouth warped into a cruel smile. 'Good job we had all that family silver to sell, eh, Uncle? The money will set us up splendidly in our new lives.' He shot Archibald a disdainful look. 'You might enjoy living like a pauper, but we certainly shall not.'

'And all those ugly paintings,' Lyla chipped in. 'Who knew they'd be worth so much.'

'Most of them hundreds of years old,' Archibald added, almost as an afterthought.

It was now clear where all the missing items from the east wing had gone. But this fact bothered Stanley much less than something else. The real Aleister was as slender as his sister and, as Stanley looked at them both, standing together side-by-side, a sudden realisation hit him. 'You're *twins*,' he gasped.

Aleister stepped out from the pile of money, pulling on smaller clothes from a stack that lay nearby. 'Well spotted, Stanley.'

'Enough!' Lyla shouted. 'There's nothing more to be done while we wait for the potion, and their whining voices are like glass in my ears. Put them in *The Hole*, Aleister.' Her eyes narrowed. '*All* of them.'

The Hole turned out to be a very small and cramped stone room beneath the altar. Inside, a row of tiny candles cast an eerie trembling light over the room from rusted brackets along one wall. Stanley watched Archibald stumble inside, Millicent at his heels.

'Don't fight,' Stanley whispered to Scarlett when Aleister approached them. Right now he wanted answers, and if speaking to Millicent out of the Cabells' earshot meant being shut in this room, then so be it.

'Ah, the young twins, I presume,' said Archibald, when Stanley and Scarlett too were pushed into The Hole, a heavy lock clunking into place behind them.

'Sleep tight,' Aleister's voice laughed on the other side of the door. Then there was silence.

Stanley watched Archibald's face. It didn't show any signs of recognising him at all.

'I'm so sorry, Stanley.' Millicent's small voice emerged from the flickering gloom. 'I know you must be thinking terrible things about us, but I promise you, none of them are true.'

'How can you say that?' Scarlett was shivering. She jerked her head towards Archibald. 'He's helping the Cabells. You both are. You're all in whatever this horrible thing is together.'

Stanley pulled Scarlett down so that they were both sitting on a low wooden bench. His eyes moved from the vacant expression on Archibald's face to the sorrowful look on Millicent's. 'That can't be right, Scarlett,' he told her gently. 'If they were helping the Cabells, why would they be locked in here with us?'

Stanley leaned closer to Millicent and when he spoke next his voice was empty of all its previous anger, 'Millicent, you have to tell us everything.'

Chapter Twenty-One

The Unfortunate Archibald Marble

Millicent jumped onto Archibald's lap. 'I promise I will, Stanley, in just a minute.' She pushed her snout into the old man's jacket pocket, removing a small leafy bundle with her teeth. Nudging his fingers open, she dropped the leaves into his hand. 'Eat up, Archie,' she said gently. 'It's your favourite.'

'Is it?' Archibald considered the contents of his hand. 'Am I hungry?'

'Oh yes, you asked me to make it for you.' She guided his hand up to his mouth.

While Archibald chewed, Scarlett gripped Stanley again. 'What did it give him,' she asked in a terrified whisper. 'What's going to happen?'

'Millicent's not an *it*,' he replied, 'she's –' But he didn't get to tell Scarlett anything more. Archibald had lurched forward,

152

expelling a long deep groan, Millicent falling, startled, from his lap.

'Mr Marble,' Stanley exclaimed, leaping up. 'Are you all right?'

Silent seconds passed before, with a loud cough, Archibald pulled himself upright. He smiled at them and, Stanley thought suddenly, looked like a much younger man.

'Ah, Millicent, my friend,' Archibald said, reaching out to stroke her with a still slightly shaking hand. 'You've always had such a wonderful memory for my recipes. An antidote, I presume, to the Befuddlement Brew they forced on me.'

Millicent's mouth stretched into a grin so wide they could see every one of her tiny white teeth. 'Yes, I remembered helping you make it; we used the book, *One Hundred Uses for Scorpion Venom.*'

A rich golden twinkle glistened in the old man's once empty eyes. 'Ah, yes, our friends the arachnids; much misunderstood creatures.'

'I couldn't make the antidote into a tea, like you did,' Millicent went on happily, 'but I thought the mixture would work just the same.'

'And how right you were.' Archibald smiled wearily, leaning back against the wall. 'Don't worry,' he said, at the look of concern on each of their faces. 'I'll regain my strength soon enough, now that I'm *me* again.' He winked. 'A few more doses of that antidote and I'll be as sprightly as an acrobat's apprentice.'

Soon the colour had returned to his cheeks and his furrowed brow relaxed. 'Stanley and Scarlett,' he said, offering them each a hand, 'it's a pleasure to meet you both *properly.*'

After Stanley had finished shaking hands, Scarlett reached for the old man's hand uncertainly. 'So, you're not really working with the Cabells?' she whispered.

'Not by choice.' The light faded from Archibald's eyes. 'You see, children, under the ruinous influence of the Befuddlement Brew, Aleister and Lyla were able to take complete control of me. My mind fogged and even my body weakened. I could only watch what I was doing from a place of entrapment, deep inside myself.' He hesitated for a moment. 'It seems I have again underestimated my niece and nephew, much to my peril. Since the day they brought me here they've had me sleepwalking through a nightmare.'

Stanley threw Scarlett a fearful look. 'Mr Marble, what did you mean earlier, about needing our bodies?'

Archibald paled under his gaze. 'Is that what I said?' Creakily, he pulled himself to his feet, giving a long laboured sigh. 'There is indeed a story to tell. An extremely unpleasant story, but one that must be told all the same.' He turned towards the wall and Stanley got the feeling that whatever he was about to say was so horrible he couldn't bring himself to look at them.

Eventually, and in low sad voice, he began. 'When my niece and nephew were children I loved them dearly. Their father had died when they were babies, and their mother, my sister Bella, brought them to visit me often. I taught them how to brew basic potions and cast simple spells. I helped them study the ancient texts.'

Stanley and Scarlett glanced at each other, both remembering Bella's grave, but as Archibald began to pace the tiny room, still refusing to meet their eyes, they wordlessly agreed that this wasn't the time to interrupt him with questions.

'The mage arts have been passed down through my family for many centuries,' Archibald went on. 'We've never been exactly sure where the *Book of Wonders* originally came from; it is an ageless thing, created in a time when magic was still part of the world, as natural as the sun and wind. The Book contains a variety of ancient spells, as well as those we created ourselves over the years; all learned from my family's years of travel, and their study of magical cultures. Bella was the first of the Marbles to go against this magical tradition. She refused to even talk about magic.'

Archibald gave another deep sigh. 'I'm ashamed to say that I taught her children in secret, and the more I showed them, the more they begged to learn.' Now, at last, he turned to look at the twins. 'By the time Aleister and Lyla were your age I had become concerned about their magical *motives*. When I finally discovered the terrible truth, it was too late.'

Archibald's eyes darkened and he closed them for a long time. Scarlett shifted closer to Stanley on the bench while they waited. When Archibald opened his eyes again he seemed to have composed himself.

'One day Aleister and Lyla slipped my sister and me a sleeping draft. They then attempted to perform a spell on us.' Archibald took a long steadying breath. 'A very dark and exceptionally complicated spell called *Anima Muto* – a ritual that allows you to place your soul into the body of another, and their soul into yours.'

The yellow of Millicent's eyes shimmered bright and scared in the candlelight.

'But who did they want to switch their souls with?' Stanley blurted, 'and *why?*'

Archibald's voice dropped, as though ashamed of the words he was about to speak. 'It seemed that Aleister and Lyla had become impatient with childhood. By using *Anima Muto* on Bella and myself, they could take our bodies and live as us, with all my magical knowledge and with the freedom of adults to live in any way they chose.'

Archibald dropped down onto the bench and grabbed his head with both hands. When he looked up again his eyes shone with tears. 'Of course the spell was much too advanced for the children, and they had not yet learned that such favours have a price.'

No one spoke as they waited for him to continue; even the room itself seemed to be holding its breath.

Archibald went on gravely. 'Performing the *Anima Muto* spell requires the conjuring and trapping of some of the most maligned and feared creatures of the Hidden Realms,'

Stanley wasn't sure how, but from somewhere, he found his voice. 'The... *where?*'

'The Hidden Realms,' Archibald repeated. 'They are not on any map because they exist at the edges of our known world; in underground caverns and hidden burrows, on remote lost islands and in caves set into the furthest mountains. In these dark and dismal spaces live the wondrous yet monstrous races.'

A terrified look twisted Scarlett's face. 'You mean those strange worlds exist now, and those creatures are actually *real?*'

As Archibald nodded, something occurred to Stanley.

'The priest hole,' he exclaimed, 'all those skulls... that *claw!*

Mr Marble, have *you* been to the Hidden Realms?'

The old man shook his head solemnly. 'My ancestors did, it was they who collected the specimens you must have seen in my workshop. I however, have no wish to go.' He shivered before continuing. 'I restrict myself to collecting rare plants and herbs, from our known world. And besides,' he fixed them all with a warning stare, 'entering these realms only helps weaken the boundaries between them and us and, believe me when I say, that is something more dangerous than you could ever imagine.'

Stanley struggled to keep the fear from his voice when he asked, 'Mr Marble, what exactly did Lyla and Aleister call out of the Hidden Realms?'

A deep struggle played over the old man's face. 'A ritual as dark as *Anima Muto* requires the aid of an exceptionally powerful creature,' he said, pausing for a long moment. 'I doubt either of *you* would be foolish enough to attempt to enslave a demon?'

Stanley almost laughed out loud at the madness of the idea, but stopped when he saw Archibald's expression. It was of coldest steel.

'There are demons in the Hidden Realms?' Scarlett asked, shakily.

'Many,' Archibald replied. 'In every hideous form. It is not surprising that things went horribly wrong. My sister was killed.' His expression showed he did not want to go into details.

Scarlett looked like she'd stopped breathing. 'What about you, Mr Marble?' she gasped. 'Weren't you hurt, too?'

Archibald reached inside his yellowing shirt and pulled out

a string with what looked like a piece of coal attached to it. 'A lodestone amulet,' he said. 'Lodestone is magically powerful in its own right, but it also attracts iron.' He held the amulet up to show the tiny flecks of metal attached to the black rock. 'Iron is the blood of the earth; it protects against many dark forces. You will find the protecting influence of iron, silver and salt all over this house. That day, iron was the thing that saved my life. Here,' he held the amulet out to Scarlett. 'You take it.'

'Thank you,' she said quietly, placing it over her head with a nervous smile.

'If only my sister and the children had been wearing one,' Archibald went on, 'but, like I say, Bella rebelled against magical things. Sadly I think it because she had very little talent in the mage arts. That's why I taught her children in secret.' His gaze turned into a pleading expression. 'Not a day goes by that I don't regret that decision.'

The words were out of Stanley's mouth before he could stop them, '*That's* why Bella doesn't have a symbol on her grave; because she was *different*,' he said. 'Not magical.'

Archibald gave a resigned nod. 'When I buried her, I couldn't bring myself to give her the *Mark of the Mage* adopted by my family. If I had only honoured her wishes and left her children without magical knowledge, she'd still be alive today, and none of this...' he broke off sadly.

'Weren't Aleister and Lyla harmed in the ritual too?' Stanley asked.

Archibald shook his head. 'Thankfully demons are seldom hungry for the souls of children. Yet while it's true that the children survived, they were certainly not unharmed by the ritual. The unquenched spell left a curse upon them. It needed something to devour to satisfy itself, so it swam in their veins and would have destroyed them from the inside out if I hadn't given them a powerful healing draught to halt its progress.'

Millicent's ears pulled back and she asked the question burning Stanley's lips. 'Why did you help them, Archie, after everything they'd done?'

'They were so young,' he exclaimed. 'The death of their mother seemed to bring them to their senses. They were terrified and ashamed. And they had been punished too; for while the healing potion prevented the curse from growing stronger, it couldn't be reversed completely.' He paused. 'For some things there can be no true cure.'

'But they *weren't* truly sorry, were they,' said Stanley. 'We wouldn't be here if they were.'

'At first I believe they were sorry,' Archibald said. 'They lived with me at Marble Manor. They became quiet, even kind children at times. When they grew up and left home they came to visit me each week, and I gave them the healing potion; I still didn't trust them enough to teach them how to make it for themselves. This went on for many years, until one day they came back asking for… *more.*'

'More potion?' asked Millicent.

'No, my little friend,' replied Archibald, 'much more than that. They told me they were afraid of being reliant on me and my secret magic, and it was soon clear they wanted to delve into the Book's darker pages once more, to find a *permanent* cure, whatever the cost might be.'

Stanley shifted on the wooden bench.

'It was then that I banished them from the house. I refused

to help them a day longer. Their time had come; I knew that I must let them die.'

'I – I don't understand,' Scarlett trembled. 'Why didn't they die?'

'It seems I have a bad habit of underestimating the ruthless determination, the all-consuming greed, of my niece and nephew,' Archibald replied sadly. 'My protective enchantments worked for a time, but eventually, only very recently in fact, they managed to get their hands on the Book.'

Stanley felt instantly cold. 'It – it was me, Mr Marble,' he said weakly. 'I told the Cabells where the book was.' He was afraid to look up, fearful of what he might see in Archibald's eyes.'

'Only because they threatened to hurt *me!*' Stanley heard Millicent tell Archibald. She jumped from his lap onto Stanley's. 'You were just protecting me,' she said, nudging him gently.

'They still got you though, didn't they?'

Archibald crossed the small space to where Stanley was sitting. 'The only thing you are guilty of, young man, is bravery and love.' He laid a hand on Stanley's shoulder. 'You are stronger than you appear to realise. You are not to blame for what has happened here. Neither is your sister.'

Stanley watched Scarlett return Archibald's smile. 'But before they found your book, how did the Cabells get *you*, Mr Marble?' she asked, her voice shaking even more now.

'One night they trapped me in my attic,' he said. 'I had protected the house from dark forces entering from outside, Lyla and Aleister included. Having been touched by a demon, they are themselves now impure.' He gazed around him sadly.

'I hadn't realised they were coming from *inside*. Why didn't I think to protect the chapel entrance?'

'So that's how they got in,' Stanley whispered, 'through the chapel into the walls of Marble Manor.' He remembered what Lyla had said about the salt too. 'And they were able to come through the front door when they visited because Dad had broken the line of protective salt.'

'When they found me they did terrible things,' Archibald went, his expression grim, 'but still I wouldn't tell them where the Book was, so they forced me to come here.' He looked thoughtful for a moment. 'It was strange, how Aleister was getting fatter, yet the mark of the curse was clear upon him. Lyla wasn't afflicted by the convulsions experienced by her brother, but the stench of the curse's consumption was strongest on her. No matter how she tried to cover it up with perfume and powders, it was obvious the curse was spreading. In its different ways the curse was destroying them both one cell at a time, their bodies breaking down, every part of them slowly dying. Without the healing potion they were becoming little more than the walking dead.'

Stanley felt a collective shudder pass over the room.

Archibald's expression grew sadder with each passing moment of his story. 'But once they'd gained possession of the Book, they were able to make the healing potion for themselves, and the Befuddlement Brew for me.'

'So that's why they are healthier now?' exclaimed Stanley.

'Yes,' Archibald replied gravely. 'But with so much damage done the curse's touch still lingers; I sense it in the air of every space they inhabit, almost as if their souls are still decaying, even if their bodies are not.' For the first time Archibald looked truly angry. 'They forced me to make *other* potions, mixtures only an adept mage like myself is capable of brewing correctly.'

'Aleister made me go to the greenhouse,' Millicent added, 'to collect what they needed. Lyla said they would hurt you and Scarlett if I tried to speak to you, so all I could think to do was get the ingredients for Archie's antidote at the same time.'

'And you rescued me,' said Archibald, stroking Millicent again.

'I'm sorry, Mr Marble,' Stanley said suddenly, 'but you're not rescued; none of us are. The Cabells have us trapped, and it seems pretty clear what you've been trying to tell us. Aleister and Lyla want to use the *Anima Muto* spell again, don't they? They're looking for two *new* bodies to put their souls into. *Our* bodies – mine and Scarlett's.'

Chapter Twenty-Two
The Body Snatchers

Stanley watched the colour drain from Scarlett's face.

'I'm so sorry, children,' Archibald said, tears springing into his eyes once more. 'That's precisely what they plan to do.'

Stanley fought the quiver in his voice when he said, 'So that means *our* souls will go into *their* cursed bodies?'

A storm passed over the old man's face. 'Yes.'

No one spoke as the horrifying realisation wrapped around them like a cloak of nightmares. Eventually Scarlett's small voice broke the silence.

'This is all my fault,' she said, gulping back tears. 'I thought Aleister and Lyla were okay. They helped me with my homework, they seemed to really like me.' Avoiding Stanley's eyes, she went on, 'It – it was nice being the centre of attention for once... but you were right about them all along, Stanley.' When she looked up her cheeks were streaked with tears. 'I... I thought you were being a baby... If I'd just listened to you... I'm so sorry, I –'

'*Stop,*' Archibald said in a low firm voice. 'The only blame here lies with my niece and nephew and... *myself*. I should never have allowed them back all those years ago; never taught them enough to permit this ghastly plan to unfold.'

Staring back at Archibald, Stanley was seized by a sudden and gut-wrenching realisation. '*That's* why the Cabells advertised Marble Manor, isn't it? It was all part of their plan; they *lured* us here.'

The door to The Hole swung open. 'How right you are, Stanley,' said Aleister, stepping inside. 'Exactly right.' His eyes lingered on both children with a prideful expression. 'My sister and I are to begin our entire lives again, so we had to find just the right set of twins.' He gave a long sigh of satisfaction. 'Imagine our joy when we found you two.' With a bony hand, Aleister reached for Stanley's face. 'That jet black hair combined with those dazzling blue eyes; why, we're a perfect match.'

Stanley shrank quickly away from Aleister's cold touch. 'There's *nothing* matching about you two and us,' he grimaced. Then, something else lurched into his thoughts. '*Mum and Dad...* what happens to them when you're living as us?'

'Well now, let me think.' A horrible smile twisted Aleister's lips. 'We won't exactly need them, not as we'll have dearest

Uncle here taking care of us, and teaching us *everything* he knows.' Aleister bent forward, holding his face an inch from Stanley's. His breath was no longer foul, but the touch of it made Stanley flinch anyway. 'We'll send them back to London with a good dose of Befuddlement Brew, they probably won't even remember they have kids.'

Stanley felt his hands coil into fists. 'You can't *make* us do this,' he screamed at Aleister.

'We'll fight you all the way!' Scarlett joined, those bright blue eyes turning steely grey.

Aleister merely smiled. 'We'll see.' He turned coolly to Archibald. 'Enough of this foolish chatter, I believe we are ready to start, Uncle.'

But the old man's cheeks had flushed with crimson. 'You evil, disgusting, vulture,' he blurted out. 'To think that you are part of my own bloodline. No, it's too much to bear…' The look of shock on Aleister's face made him break off suddenly.

'You're *y–you* again,' Aleister spluttered. 'But how?' He glared at each of their silent faces, steeling himself when no reply came. 'No matter, I'll deal with you, and that *rat* later.' He snarled at Millicent before turning to Stanley and Scarlett. 'Once the ritual is complete.'

'Aleister, wait,' Archibald's tone was much gentler this time. Reaching out slowly, he touched his nephew's arm. 'You don't have to do this. Keep taking the healing potion and you'll have more years of life, and maybe I can formulate something else; something that can –'

'Cure us completely?' Aleister shook his uncle away. 'We both know it can't be done. Now get out. *All* of you!'

One by one, Aleister dragged them into the chapel, where an incredible scene met their eyes – Lyla was seated, cross-legged, inside a burning circle of lit candles, a jewelled bowl sparkling by her feet. She was turning something Stanley couldn't quite see over in her hands. Hands that were covered with a pair of strange gloves that sparkled like the surface of a deep black lake.

A cold glimmer shone in Lyla's eyes when she opened those gloved hands to reveal what she was holding.

'What is it?' Stanley hissed, as Archibald gave a low moan. The object was long and curved like a horn, but with a point as sharp as a dagger. It glistened in the dancing candlelight like some deep red gemstone.

'My dragon fang,' Archibald breathed.

'*Our* dragon fang,' Lyla replied, stroking it with one long gloved finger. 'What's yours is ours now, remember, Uncle.' She held up her other hand examining the glistening glove. Black ripples moved over its surface like liquid. 'Good job *we* also now own a pair of dragon-tongue gloves.'

'A dragon fang burns like flame,' Archibald murmured to the twins, 'even once extracted, and dragon's tongue is impervious to dragon flame.'

Stanley's skin prickled at the very thought, but his body was burning with its own kind of flame – the irresistible urge to fight. Not wasting another second, he kicked backwards at Aleister, scraping his heel along Aleister's shin.

'Run!' Stanley yelled, leaping towards the chapel door; Aleister crying out in pain. Stanley grabbed the door handle, turning and pulling with everything he had.

In a heartbeat Scarlett was beside him, her hands on his.

They shook the handle together, their feet kicking the door as one.

'Help! Anyone! Please, help us!' Scarlett screamed.

Of course the door was locked, but that didn't matter. Their will to fight, to survive, was stronger than some ancient slab of wood – if they could just pull hard enough. Stanley's heart leapt when the handle shuddered – the lock was loosening.

'You really don't want to do that.' A note of triumph had rung through Aleister's voice.

Scarlett turned, trembling, 'Stanley, stop… *look!*'

With a sickening feeling in the pit of his stomach, Stanley followed Scarlett's terrified stare. Archibald was in the middle of the burning circle, his body buckled with fear at the sight of the dragon's fang hovering barely millimetres from his face. Millicent shivered by Archibald's feet, she too struck dumb with fear. There was nothing either of them could do; wherever Archibald turned the fang followed.

Stanley looked wildly around, giving a loud gasp; Lyla was controlling the fang from her place on the floor. Twirling those sparkling black fingers, her cruel mouth mumbled strange words that Stanley knew must be a spell from the Book.

Yet, Stanley soon realised, Lyla wasn't the only one using magic. Through barely moving lips, Archibald was muttering his own words. But while Archibald Marble was possessed of what was probably the most powerful Marble blood there was, it was clear to Stanley that he was still too weak to counter Lyla's spell with his own magic, and the fang remained dangerously close to his throat.

Very slowly, Stanley lifted his hands away from the door handle.

'That's more like it,' Aleister said, drinking in the fear Stanley knew must be carved onto his face.

'You must leave me, children,' Archibald cried suddenly. 'Take Millicent and run, I have no fear of... *AAARGH!*'

A horrible sizzling sound accompanied Archibald's cry of pain. For just a moment, and squealing with enjoyment, Lyla had touched the dragon fang against the soft skin of the old man's neck. Stanley and Scarlett watched aghast as a patch of angry blisters burst out over Archibald's skin.

Stanley had never felt so helpless. How could two children, a hurt old man and a timid fox, possibly overpower the evil Cabells, renewed to full health and armed with magic?

Millicent, it seemed, had other ideas. '*No one – hurts – MY ARCHIE!*' she screamed, tears of fury flying from her eyes as she ran at Lyla.

Shrieking, Lyla dropped the dragon fang, but in the same moment Millicent stopped dead in her tracks. To everyone's shock and surprise, Aleister had started singing. The words of the song were strange and hypnotic and Stanley watched in fearful fascination as the snarl in Millicent's snout slackened, her eyes staring straight ahead, faded yellow and unblinking.

Now the song's tone turned high and mocking and Millicent rose into the air, Aleister twirling his fingers just like Lyla had when controlling the fang, so that, soon, the poor fox was spinning helplessly above them.

'The *Song of Sirenum*,' Aleister said. 'Of course, it's slightly more difficult manipulating *living* objects than inanimate ones.' He shot a sideways glance at the fang with a superior smirk. 'But much more fun.' Closing his eyes, Aleister's head swayed in time with the music. 'Isn't it beautiful? Sirenum laps at your very soul and –'

'– Stop now, brother,' Lyla said sulkily. 'No need to show off.'

Aleister's eyes snapped open, but he didn't stop singing; guiding Millicent towards him with an amused expression. Then, abruptly, he stopped; Millicent dropping from the air like a shot pheasant, straight into his waiting arms. Flashing a nasty grin at Archibald, Aleister was soon humming the song again, just loud enough to keep a whimpering Millicent still.

Lyla meanwhile had got to her feet. 'Well then,' she said, picking up the dragon fang in one hand, the jewelled bowl in the other. 'Now that the heroics are over with, perhaps you'd care to cast your eyes over the potion, Uncle. Is it ready?'

Peering closer, Stanley recognised the bowl's dark purple liquid at once. It was the potion Archibald had completed earlier that night. Except now the mixture was silent, its oily surface flat and unmoving.

'And don't even think about lying to us, Uncle,' Aleister growled. He began stroking Millicent with a bony finger. 'Not only do I have your friend here, but you know it'll be much worse for the children if the mixture's been made incorrectly.'

'Yes,' Lyla chimed in with her own icy warning. 'I'm sure you don't want these innocent children going the same way as our poor dear mother.'

Sorrow clouded Archibald's eyes as he stepped forwards and looked into the bowl. With a reluctant nod he dropped to his knees. 'Please, please don't do this,' he begged. 'Search inside yourselves, I know there's a part of you that's sorry for what happened to Bella. Don't make the same mistake again. Your guilt will eat away at you more than the curse ever could. You've had your lives, now let the children have theirs.'

Shaking her head Lyla gave a long sigh, and began walking around the circle. 'Come now, Uncle, be truthful; is that *really* what you want?' she asked with a crooked smile. 'All you had to do to prevent these things from happening was rip the dark spells out of the Book. Tear them up. Burn them. *Anything* to destroy them. But you never did. Why is that, I wonder?'

'You cannot rip a page from a b–book of this p–power,' Archibald stammered. 'Such a thing would… *anger* it.'

'Or is that what you tell yourself?' Lyla's smile had become a leering slit in her face. 'Would you like to know what I think, Uncle? I think that secretly you wanted to put the Book's true power to the test, and *that's* why you left it intact.'

'Never!' Archibald gasped. 'I would sooner throw it into the fire than see you use it to steal these children's futures.'

With a cynical laugh Lyla said, 'Wasting such a magnificent object on trifling spells is the real insult to its power. The time has come for you to witness the true extent of what this book of terrible wonders can do.' Placing both bowl and fang carefully back on the floor, she pulled off a glove.

'Are you sure you don't want me to do it?' Aleister said suddenly.

'No' Lyla replied, with an odd smile. 'Save yours for *later.*' And now she took a small dagger from her pocket, wincing slightly when she pressed its tip into her own finger. Stanley winced too as a shimmering pearl of blood sprung up there.

'Stop, Lyla…*please!*' Archibald cried, desperately. 'You

don't know how to control it. Look what happened last time.'

'The only mistake we made last time was trusting an inferior demon,' she yelled back.

'Don't worry, old man,' Aleister sneered. 'Things are going to be very different this time.'

Stanley's pulse throbbed. Lyla was holding out her crimson-tipped hand towards the altar. 'Ancient and wondrous Book of Light and Shadows,' she called, 'the Blood of the Mage calls you.'

'Death will find you in the end,' Archibald cried. 'Even if you succeed this time. You can't hide from it forever.'

Except for a pitying laugh, Lyla ignored him; calling to the Book much more loudly, and this time in the Book's own language. With each new word she spoke the candles shimmered brighter, their flames a sea of dancing colours that Stanley would have found astonishing to watch, if he wasn't just about to have his soul sucked from his body.

Slowly the Book rose up from the altar. It floated through the air towards Lyla, falling softly into her outstretched arms. With a terrible grin, she allowed a single shining pearl of her own blood to drip onto the Book's cover. Then, pulling in a long trembling breath, she whispered, '*Anima Muto.*'

The Book opened in her hands, its pages rustling for a long moment until, eventually, it lay still.

Lyla turned to her brother, her breath coming fast and shallow. 'Can you believe it's really happening, Aleister, after all these years?'

Clapping both hands to his mouth, Aleister let Millicent drop to the floor. He ran to join his sister, each of their cruel joyful faces transfixed for a moment on the other's.

Archibald's gaze found Stanley's. The old man's eyes widened before moving from Millicent to the door. Stanley could feel the plea stretching towards him. Archibald wanted the children to run, to take Millicent and save themselves. This time, Archibald would see his niece and nephew's wickedness through to the very end, whatever it cost him.

But Millicent had jumped into his arms, where she lay protectively across his chest. The move told Stanley what deep down he already knew; that Millicent would rather die than be without her Archie.

As Stanley watched silent tears fill the deep lines of the old man's face, he knew that even if it was somehow possible to escape, he would never abandon Archibald and Millicent to these monsters. One glance at Scarlett told him she felt the same.

And now, watching each of them in turn, a new hope rose in Stanley's chest. Archibald was weak, yes, but he was still an expert magician; Millicent was brave as well as cunning, and Stanley and Scarlett, well, they may be small but they were learning more about Marble Manor's secret magic every moment. There *must* be a way to overturn this hideous plan. They just needed to work together.

'It's time,' Aleister said, turning suddenly to the children.

Lyla's cold voice joined her brother's. 'Come, *now!*'

Stanley's eyes still fixed on Scarlett, he drew in a long, determined breath, his silent lips forming the question, *ready?*

She looked terrified, but nodded.

Stanley reached for her hand and, together, they walked into the fiery circle.

Chapter Twenty-Three

Web of Dreams

Aleister and Lyla's gleeful gazes lapped hungrily over the children. Aleister even licked his lips.

Archibald's face was deathly pale, his voice a tremble of emotion when he said, 'Oh children what have you done?'

'It isn't over yet,' Stanley said, staring defiantly at both Cabells.

'Oh, I think you'll find it is.'

Stanley and Scarlett moved closer together; the ice in Lyla's voice was enough to chill the air around them.

But Archibald seemed to be mustering his strength.

Colour was rising in those white cheeks, his eyes shining like burnished gold. Pulling himself up to his fullest height, he addressed his niece and nephew with something new in his voice. 'You may be of Marble blood, but the Book of Wonders is mine more than it will ever be yours, and I'll prove it.' His soft eyes sharpened into an unflinching stare. 'Light over Shade,' he cried, 'hear my call! The Heart of the Mage calls you!'

At the old man's words both Aleister and Lyla shook their heads with relaxed smiles.

'Don't waste your breath, Uncle,' Aleister sighed. 'The Book has already shown us its allegiance.'

'It prefers the powerful over the feeble,' Lyla added cruelly.

Ignoring this, Archibald began to chant in the Book's own language, just as Lyla had done before him. Stanley felt Scarlett's hand squeezing his. The *Book of Wonders* was rising into the air, and moving towards Archibald much more quickly than it had done with Lyla.

Lyla's face crumpled in dismay, while Aleister's twisted in fury. With an owl-like screech he ran at Archibald, knocking him clean off his feet with a sickening crunch of bone on stone floor. Shoving Millicent aside, Aleister knelt on Archibald's chest, until the old man's breathing turned to a shallow jagged wheeze.

Stanley lunged towards them, but was stopped in his tracks; Scarlett holding him back by his t-shirt.

'Don't be stupid,' she hissed through gritted teeth. 'Lyla still has the fang!'

'She won't harm us,' Stanley hissed back. 'Not if she wants our bodies!'

'No, but she'll hurt Archie or Mill –'

The rest of the word dropped from Scarlett's open mouth. Millicent had sprung onto Aleister's back, her claws drawing out fat pearls of blood as she sunk them deep into the pale skin of his neck; the combined yells of man and fox blending in a deafening echo that tolled like a great bell around the chapel.

'Oh no you don't!' Lyla was upon them, but Stanley's heart leapt. In her haste to grab Millicent, she'd let go of the dragon's fang. The sight of it just lying there, forgotten on the floor, was almost too much to bear, and Stanley hopped on the spot, heart thumping as his mind raced; how could he get hold of it without the gloves?

Lyla's furious cries soon chased the thought from his head. The crazed woman was pulling a startled Millicent by the tail, shrieking, 'Get away from my brother... *now!*'

Scarlett screamed, as Millicent came flying through the air towards them. Leaping into position, Stanley caught the thrown and flailing fox before she hit the ground. The impact sent him reeling backwards, but he managed to keep his balance.

Breathing quickly, he looked down at Millicent, fearful of what damage Lyla might have done her. To his great surprise, she gazed up at him with a broad smile on her face.

A second later he saw why. The *Book of Wonders* was floating gently towards them. Stanley and Scarlett exchanged a knowing look; Archibald must have intended the Book to come to *them* all along; deliberately using himself as a decoy. And however frightening it was to see Lyla and Aleister now both wrestling the frail old man on the other side of the circle,

Archie's plan had worked. Opening her arms, Scarlett caught the Book with a tiny yelp of excitement.

Lyla ran to the table, grabbing armfuls of a strange plant from the pile of greenery Millicent had been working with earlier.

'The Witch's Hair,' Stanley gasped, suddenly recognising the protective vines from Archibald's attic.

'Nothing like using your own weapons against you,' Aleister snorted, tying the vines tight around his uncle's thin wrists.

Leaving poor Archibald in such despicable hands, even for a second, was the last thing Stanley wanted to do, but Archie had sacrificed himself to buy them valuable time. There was no choice but to pay him back with an escape plan; they just needed one fast. '*Come on,*' Stanley told himself. '*Think!*'

As though obeying his command, a blood red shimmer caught his attention. It was the fang, glinting in the firelight, and still abandoned on the chapel floor. *Of course, dragons!* Excitement flooded him. Even though the fang's fiery protection meant it was only the Cabells who could use it, there was nothing stopping Stanely from using dragon's *breath*.

He looked down at Millicent. 'We have to set the Jinx off, like *last time!*' he said in an urgent whisper. 'The fire and smoke will hide us like last time; remember what Lyla said when she came into my room – they think the flames are *real!* When they're distracted we can find the potion bowl, tip it over. They can't perform the ritual without it!'

Scarlett looked confused but Millicent nodded eagerly.

'Quick!' Stanley told Scarlett, pulling the Book open. 'We

need a spell... or a potion recipe... *anything* written in English so we can say it right.'

Quickly, Millicent leapt onto his shoulder, allowing the twins to easily turn the pages.

'*Here's one!*' Stanley stabbed at the page in front of them; Scarlett reading aloud, 'A *Dreaming Draft...*'

'Keep going,' he urged her. 'Read quietly but clearly, okay?'

She nodded and, together, in low steady voices, they began to read – 'Mix ten crocodile tears with one drop of mandrake oil and a pinch of vampire dust. Stir in a set of faery wings – *faery wings* –' Scarlett cried, horrified. 'Shhh,' Stanley warned, 'keep reading!'

But Aleister had wheeled around, giving a roar of anger at the sight of the Book in their hands.

'Add ten Jujube thorns...' they read on hurriedly,

'Finish tying him up,' Aleister barked at Lyla, before springing towards them.

'Sprinkle with werewolf fur and –'

'AAARGH!' With an almighty bellow, Aleister was upon them, tugging at the Book with all his angry might.

He was too late. Stanley gave a loud, joyful whoop: smoke was pouring from the Book's pages, flames curling the parchment edges. He could feel the Dragon's Breath Jinx growing in strength with each new pound of his heart. Soon the entire chapel would be filled with smoke and purple flame.

'What's happening?' Scarlett screamed, dropping the Book as it became too hot to hold.

'The Book won't allow anyone of non-Marble blood to use it,' Stanley explained. Pulling off his top, he used it to grasp the Book. 'It's setting of a protection jinx.' He dropped his voice to barely a whisper. 'Don't worry, the flame's aren't real... just meant to scare us.'

Under a vast cloak of smoke and flame, they stepped silently backwards and away from Aleister, concealed from his searching gaze.

'After three, we run!' Stanley hissed. 'Remember, the flames can't harm you... okay... one, two, *three!*'

And so they ran. Hot wax burned Stanley's ankle as he kicked over a candle, but they didn't stop until they could no longer see Aleister's outline. Reaching through the haze, Stanley pulled Scarlett and Millicent closer. 'Millicent, you find Archie, bite through those vines. I'll find the bowl, spill the potion.'

'Aleister! Where are you?' Lyla's voice had come from somewhere too close for Stanley's liking.

'Quickly, get this out of here.' He thrust the wrapped up Book into Scarlett's hands. 'That old door handle loosened earlier; shake it for all its worth and I bet it'll open!'

'I don't want to leave you,' she murmured.

'We'll find you, I promise.'

Scarlett gave a shiver, but did as he asked. Using the Book to waft the smoke from her eyes, she tiptoed away from him in search of the chapel door.

'Okay, Millicent, try to find Archie... *Millicent?*' No reply came and with a cold start Stanley realised that she was gone from his shoulder.

'Come out, come out, wherever you are.'

Slowly, he turned towards the chilling sound of Lyla's voice. It was closer this time, much closer. And now he caught a glimpse of that leering face looming through the smoke. Even worse was the sight of the dragon fang, held up threateningly before her.

Stanley stumbled backwards, and in his haste to get away, tripped, landing with a cry of pain on his backside.

'*There* you are.'

At first Lyla's grin was triumphant, but soon it warped into a startled grimace. She was staring at something above Stanley's head, those blue eyes stretched wide, like two of Mum's best dinner plates.

Stanley glanced behind him. '*Millicent!*' he breathed, steeling backwards as the fox came hurtling over his head, wrapped inside a halo of that swirling purple flame. '*Yes!*' He cried aloud. Millicent was magically bound to the Dragon's Breath Jinx, just like on the first day he'd seen her. Except, *this time,* the fox's claws were reaching out for Lyla, flexed in terrible fury.

With a piercing cry from both of them, Millicent hit a gobsmacked Lyla at full speed, sending her reeling across the stone floor. Lyla banged her head hard as she landed and, completely dazed and for a second time, the fang fell from her hand with a loud clang.

'That'll teach you to throw *me* around!' Millicent yelled down at her.

'*Stanley!*' Scarlett's cry came to him thin and terrified. Scrambling to his feet, he searched desperately for her through the smoke. It had begun to clear, and Stanley saw Millicent reach Archie, biting through the witch's hair that bound him with her sharp little teeth. But there was no sign of Scarlett.

'Stanley, *help!* I'm over here!'

Turning on the spot again, at long last he saw her. She was by the door. And not alone. Panic lurched in Stanley's stomach: Scarlett and Aleister were playing a horrible game of cat and mouse; Aleister making a lunge for the Book every few seconds, Scarlett only just managing to evade his grasp each time.

Then came a soft murmuring. It sounded like Archibald. They all heard it, turning as one to see the dragon fang floating through the air again; except it was Archibald controlling it now, and rather than using it to threaten anyone, he was guiding it towards the chapel window.

A storm raged in Aleister's eyes, while Archibald's expression was almost cheerful. Clearly this new turn of events was reviving the old man's strength. Just as clear was the struggle on Aleister's face. He stared from the Book to the fang, and back again, his torment as visible as that twirling black moustache. How could he decide which of these two magical objects he needed most at this very moment?

Hissing at Scarlett, he released his grip on the Book, opting for the fang, and running at Archibald with hands stretched towards the old man's mouth.

Not taking his eyes from Alesteir, Archibald spoke faster and the dragon fang gave a sudden burst of speed. With a splintering crash it shattered the chapel window on its journey out into the night.

Stanley and Scarlett whooped with delight, but their joy quickly dissolved; Archibald had crumpled to the floor in a heap, exhausted. Millicent let out a terrified squeal.

'We need to get him out of here,' Stanley croaked. 'Before

it's too late.'

'But how?' Scarlett exclaimed, watching Millicent nudging and licking his face to no avail.

'You old fool!' Aleister raged ruthlessly at Archibald. 'No one is going to stop us this time. *No one.* Do you hear me? We are destined to use the *Anima Muto. Destined!*' He spat the last word onto his uncle. 'And there's nothing you can do to stop us!'

Well there *was* something Stanley could do. Not wasting another second, he ran to Scarlett, pulling the Book open again. 'There must be a spell in here we can use against them,' he said, scanning the pages. 'And if the Jinx goes off again, all the better.' He turned the pages faster. 'Yes, *look!* Here's a –'

'– *Chorus Arenea!*' Aleister screamed suddenly over Stanley's words.

The curse hit him like an electric shock; his words swallowed by what felt like a large and sticky ball of cotton wool in his throat. A ball that began to swell.

'Learnt that one by heart last night,' Aleister said with a nasty laugh.

Choking and wheezing, Stanley couldn't reply; more alarmingly, he could no longer breathe.

'What have you done?' Scarlett yelled at Aleister, slapping Stanley desperately on the back. Aleister merely flicked a knowing eyebrow in reply.

Even with Scarlett thumping his back harder and harder, Stanley was sure his lungs were about to implode through lack of air. Then, finally, with a painful wheeze, the substance came up.

He choked again, this time in horror. Balls of thick wet

spiders' webs were glistening in his open palms.

'I'm... okay...' He spluttered. 'Get... the... potion...'

But Scarlett was trembling. 'There's sp–spiders... c–coming out of your m– mouth...'

Stanley shuddered, feeling their tiny legs crawling over his face. With a muffled cry, he tried to bat them off, but his throat was filling with more of the foul stuff and he struggled to manage even short, shallow breaths. His lungs screamed, the edges of his vision dimmed. Dropping to his knees the Book fell from his shaking hands.

So close to suffocation, Stanley didn't notice Aleister throwing witch's hair around a statue-like Scarlett, her entire body frozen with fear. Likewise, he saw nothing of Lyla, waking up and falling on the Book with greedy hands. He was barely even aware of Millicent reaching into his mouth with her tiny paws, and dragging out great lumps of web amidst fearful whimpers.

Soon a great pile of gloopy white mess lay beside Stanley and he found himself awake, gulping down long grateful breaths.

'Such a baby,' Lyla said, lazily turning the Book's pages.

With the Book of Wonders back in Marble hands, the effects of the Dragon's Breath Jinx had now burned out completely. Staggering slightly, Stanley got to his feet, able at last to see the terrible scene that lay before him.

'Let the final act begin,' Aleister said, his cruel eyes dancing.

Chapter Twenty-Four

Anima Muto

Stanley stared around the circle, fear growing inside him like a poisonous weed. Scarlett sat sobbing, tightly bound in a knot of Witch's Hair; Archibald beside her, untied, but groaning, and too weak to lift his head. Lyla had begun walking around the circle, relighting the knocked-over candles with a gleeful expression, while Aleister keep a firm and furious grip on the Book. Lastly, there was Millicent, clinging to Stanley's legs and repeating over and over again, 'What are we going to do? Oh, what are we going to do?'

They were trapped and Stanley knew it. Their time was up

and there was no longer anything he could do about it.

'Whatever happens stay with Archie,' he whispered, crouching down beside Millicent. 'Keep as safe as you can, and look after the old man when we're… we're…'

'*No*, Stanley!' she breathed. 'You *can't!*' But when he fixed her with a steely stare, she gave a weak nod of acceptance. Tears in her eyes and tail drooping, she slinked off to where Archie lay.

'Good decision, Stanley.'

He felt his hands pulled roughly behind his back by Aleister, the Witch's Hair soon so tight against his skin it burned.

'Sit down,' Lyla hissed, pushing Stanley towards Scarlett, where she sat with lips trembling and shining tears rolling down her cheeks.

'It's okay,' Stanley murmured, but he heard his own voice, empty of belief; nothing about this was okay.

'How could I have let this happen?' Archie's pitiful voice found them, and Stanley watched him force his pale face upwards to look in their direction. 'I'm so sorry, children.'

'Enough of this nonsense,' Aleister barked, dragging Archibald to his feet. Deaf to his uncle's groans, he forced the old man, stumbling, to a stone pillar just outside the circle of candles. Here, Aleister shoved Archibald to the floor, propping him up roughly against the pillar. Millicent climbed protectively onto her friend's lap with a reproachful glare.

'Now for you two!'

Stanley refused to meet Aleister's eyes as he forced him to sit cross-legged and facing Scarlett in the very centre of the circle. 'It's time to begin.' He turned to his sister. 'The potion,

Lyla. You first.'

She didn't say a word, just picked up the jewelled bowl, staring at Stanley and Scarlett for a long moment; clearly revelling in every second of this terrible victory. Finally, she took a long drink of the potion, grimacing slightly before passing the bowl to Aleister, who swallowed a large mouthful himself.

Aleister's face hardened. 'Your turn,' he said, dancing towards the children with a wicked gleam in his eyes. He grabbed Stanley first, pressing a bony hand against Stanley's forehead, until his head was forced backwards. The appalling mixture, purple and putrid, slid down Stanley's throat. It was sour and slimy and sickness swept through him the moment it reached his stomach.

'No, please... I *can't...*' Terrified, Scarlett's lips pressed together at Aleister's approached.

'Who'd have thought it'd be *you* who turned out to be the scaredy cat of the pair,' he laughed nastily.

With wretched sobs, Scarlett's mouth was forced open, and she too swallowed the potion.

'I'm with you,' Stanley whispered to her. 'It'll be over soon.'

'Oh how touching,' Lyla crowed. 'You'll be such a comfort to each other in your old age.'

Meanwhile, Aleister had stepped out of the circle again and, reaching the altar, his spidery fingers landed on the basket of eggs. Soon a pile of mottled turquoise shells piled up – Aleister had broken egg upon egg into the stone bowl.

'They – They're... *crows'* eggs!' Stanley heard Archibald gasp, and there was a definite note of panic in his voice.

'Quite right.' Aleister turned with a satisfied smile. 'We fed the crows from your insect stores, Uncle, kept them coming to the Manor in their hundreds.' Now he held a hand out to Lyla, who placed the dagger in his open palm. 'So we had the pick of the ripest eggs.'

Scarlett began to cry when Aleister pricked each of his fingers and both thumbs with the dagger, carefully dripping ten shiny pearls of blood into the bowl, which he then carried back into the circle.

Archibald's breath blew hard and fast. Aleister was now walking around the circle, pouring drops of the gloopy mixture into the candle flames. Each time a drop fell the candle's light grew brighter and stronger, until the circle was a blazing ring of brightly-coloured flames that burned the air around them.

When every candle was ablaze with strange and dazzling colour, Lyla took the bowl and crouched down. Dipping a finger inside it she began to write something on the stone floor with the thick violet liquid that was the combination of crows' eggs and Aleister's blood. She might have been dipping an old-fashioned quill into a pot of ink. Stanley recognised some of the symbols she was drawing from the pages of the Book.

He blinked. The symbols were blurring. Or was it his eyes? He tried to focus, but the room was dancing under a scatter of coloured lights, and a strange pinching sensation moved from his stomach to his chest, spreading through the rest of his body like a tiny hand feeling its way around his insides, squeezing everything it came across.

'Don't lose focus,' he heard Aleister tell Lyla. She'd fallen clumsily onto her backside and seemed to be swaying slightly, in time with the room. 'You know it'll pass if you fight it.'

Stanley glanced up. Aleister was holding himself still in the dancing light, although it looked to be taking some effort.

Scarlett gave a little cry and whispered, 'Stanley…'

It was a struggle lifting his head to face her, but somehow he managed it. She was lying on her side with her eyelids half closed. Stanley blinked again. Her face was a dancing mass of colour that he was becoming lost inside. His own eyelids closed. Everything felt dark and peaceful. All he wanted was to sleep.

Then from somewhere far away came the sound of a rich, kind voice. It reached for him through the haze, creeping through his ears to his bones, his heart. Stanley latched onto the sound, allowing that soft voice to pull at his senses until his eyes snapped open.

The voice belonged to Archibald Marble. The swirling haze was gone and Stanley could see the old man clearly. He was straining to read Lyla's violet writing, a terrified stare consuming his face.

'*Astaroth?*' he yelled suddenly. 'You have the arrogance, the *stupidity*, to conjure a *Fire Lord*; worse, *The* Fire Lord. Even if you succeed in this monstrous ritual, the price will be fearsome and inescapable.'

Lyla's cold eyes flashed back at Archibald, and Stanley was sure he'd caught a glimmer of fear in them. But the next moment she turned away from him again, calling out, loud and sure, 'Astaroth, whose light burns with Darkest flame, the blood of a Dark Heart calls you.' Lyla's body began to sway and Stanley could sense a change in the air around him. Now her voice grew loud and deep, the air pressure building with each new repetition of the command, 'Astaroth, the blood of a Dark Heart calls you.'

From where he stood, Aleister began to sway too. 'It's coming,' he said. 'Can you feel the energy, sister?'

Lyla stopped reading, her eyes travelling over the flames that surrounded them. Stanley followed her triumphant gaze to a shape moving through the candle flames, and felt his heart turn to stone then crack open. It was a face, yet barely so; the skin deathly white, almost translucent, with something dark moving beneath it. And the eyes; two holes that burned with black fire. Stanley's body gave a sickening shiver; feeling that to look too deeply into those eyes would take you to a place from which you could never return.

It was a demon's face, Stanley had no doubt, and it was growing larger within the fire, which in turn had become a deep and brilliant red. Smouldering sparks burst from the flames.

'Aleister, get the tablet!' Archibald screamed suddenly, pure terror reinvigorating him this time. 'You've learned the Runes, now read them out!'

As if awakening from a trance, Aleister leapt through the flaming circle, grabbing the stone tablet from the altar in one swift movement.

'How could you forget such a thing?' Archibald cried, his face now completely drained of blood.

Holding the tablet towards the flames, Aleister marched around the inside of the circle, calling out in a loud but slightly wavering voice, 'Magec's Light surrounds us. Branwen's Love enfolds us. Soteria's Power protects us.'

Lyla's voice also trembled when she spoke next, but she

didn't stop for a second. 'Astaroth, this rite strengthens and binds you. Rise up from your Lake of Fire and obey our command!'

There was a thunderous roar and it felt as though all the oxygen had been sucked from the room. The hungry flames rose as one, flying together to make a gigantic, scorching fire that hovered above their heads, consuming the air around them.

'Please, you must stop!' Archibald's voice rang out through the roar. 'Summoning Astaroth will mean the end for all of us!'

A scream sat paralysed in Stanley's throat. A huge, burning figure was emerging from the flames above them; a creature whose horned head scraped the ceiling of the chapel, a pair of fiery wings splayed out behind it. The smile on Lyla's face waivered as the demon floated down, standing terrible yet mesmerizing inside the circle of now spent candles.

It turned to the Cabells with its grotesque face contorted with rage, and Stanley saw with horror what was moving beneath its skin. Snakes. Small and black they writhed in continual motion, like they might burst free at any moment.

The Cabells stood before the demon, clinging to each other with one hand, using the other to each hold onto the stone tablet. Hands shaking, they raised the tablet up towards the demon.

'Astaroth – We – Command – You!' Lyla's voice had lost some of its earlier strength but her expression was determined. 'Unleash your cursed treasures upon us!'

Aleister joined in when she began to chant, '*Anima Muto, Anima Muto…*'

The demon's hollow eyes looked like two bottomless pits capable of sucking each and every one of them into its fiery depths. Stanley strained against his ties, but they only grew tighter. Scarlett looked close to fainting when the demon's black mouth opened wide and began twisting in its head. It was yelling furiously, yet the sound was distorted, like it was screaming under water.

Fear faded from Lyla's eyes as she watched the Demon's bulging body; the spell not allowing it to break free from its magical binding.

Aleister stepped forward, grabbing Stanley and dragging him into position so that they were standing directly in front of the demon. The Cabells' voices grew louder and more confident with each repetition of the chant, '*Anima Muto, Anima Muto, Anima Muto!*'

Focusing his glinting gaze on Stanley, Aleister let out a victorious cry before grasping Stanley's face in both hands. The sickening realisation of what was about to happen gripped Stanley, as Aleister kissed him hard on the lips.

Chapter Twenty-Five
The Spider's Kiss

A flash of blinding light and Stanley was pitched forward onto the ground. The pain of landing face first on solid stone was nothing compared to the crushing weight now pinning him to the floor. He couldn't move, or even breathe; not an inch of space remained inside his lungs from that invisible downward force. Then with startling suddenness, he was propelled into the air.

All pain left him as he hung there, weightless and free. There was no need to breathe when you were made entirely of light and air. It was the most wonderful sensation; every fear gone, every question wordlessly answered.

Stanley gazed at the beautiful shimmering light that had replaced his skin. His limbs were no longer bound and he could see through them to the floor beneath; to the two bodies lying there, pale and unmoving.

Wait. Wasn't one of them *his* body? *His* chest lying flat and still. *His* eyes staring back at him, empty and lifeless.

'It's working!' Lyla stepped into view, her upturned face a mask of triumph. She wasn't staring at Stanley though, and a shiver rippled through the liquid of his body; Aleister was beside him, he too a fluid and shining thing, floating in the air with him.

Lyla laughed now. It was a cruel and pitiless sound. 'I can see them, Aleister, your *souls,'* she cried. 'It's extraordinary, the spell, it's working; your souls have been *pushed out!'*

Somewhere inside him Stanley felt a tugging sensation and was soon gliding through the air. The same thing was happening to Aleister, their two souls dancing around each other in a whirlpool of light, each moment drawing closer together. Stanley tried to resist, but he had no control and the dance continued. All the while he could feel the sensation growing; like being pulled backwards inside a catapult until, with a fantastic jolt, he was flung downwards. Everything around him blurred and turned suddenly black.

Stanley knew he was back on the floor. His body felt sure and solid, and heavy; too heavy. Opening his eyes, light crept in through large blinking eyelids. There was a sting in his fingers and he raised two hands that were full-size and bloodied at the fingertips. His scream perished as soon as it hit the air; the sound frightening him. It was deep and rasping.

Not his own voice at all, more like...

'*Aleister!*' Archibald sobbed. 'How could you do this?'

Stanley pulled himself up and saw Scarlett staring back at him; her face a sickly shade.

Then his own voice rang through the air. 'Not a single ache or pain. Oh, how wondrous to be young again.'

Stanley hauled himself up onto his now long, unsteady legs, terror gripping his heart. Very slowly, he turned to face the nightmare that he knew was standing behind him.

'My, my, Stanley, how you've grown.'

It was like looking into a mirror, except with Aleister's expression of gleeful venom staring back at him in Stanley's own face.

Lyla lifted Aleister into her arms, easily now that he wore Stanley's skin. She twirled her brother around, tears flowing over her cheeks as she cried, 'It all starts here. The world is ours, yours and mine.'

When Scarlett gave a wretched sob, Stanley knelt down to comfort her. She recoiled slightly but allowed him to put Aleister's arms around her.

'The demon!' Archibald yelled suddenly. 'You must control it!'

Stanley and Scarlett both let out gasps of horror at the sight of Astaroth's flaming form. The demon was bulging and swelling more than ever inside its invisible cage. He knew he was no match for this terrible creature, but Stanley moved to put himself between it and Scarlett.

'It can't get out, you idiot,' Lyla leered. 'It's enslaved, bound in magical flame by our rightful power.'

Aleister spat his next words out like sour milk. 'You have

no idea what it takes to be a true mage, Uncle. The proof of our ability stands before you.' He gestured to his new body.

It was strange and frightening for Stanley to hear his own voice speaking these words, to see his own body moving but with another life controlling it. But more terrifying even than that was the frenzy of rage that was the demon's diabolical face. Stanley was relieved to see that, despite Aleister's brave talk, he hadn't let go of the protection tablet and kept it pointed all the while at Astaroth.

'You must keep reciting the Runes!' Archibald cried. 'Only the mage who conjures the demon can say them, you should know that!'

'Oh do be quiet, Uncle,' Lyla sighed. 'Your voice is becoming tiresome.'

Archibald gave a bellow of despair, but Lyla ignored him, turning her attention to Scarlett instead. '*My* turn,' she said.

It was sudden and overwhelming; a powerful and livid hatred overtook Stanley. He watched the panic flash in Lyla's eyes as he ran at her, knocking her sideways with all his new adult strength. 'You didn't think of *this,* did you,' Stanley hissed, pinning Lyla's arms behind her back. 'I'm not a *weedy little kid a*nymore.'

'Look, Stanley - *Aleister!*' Archibald yelled. 'Stop him!'

Stanley spun around. Aleister was running towards Scarlett with the dagger they'd used to prick their fingers. Stanley let go of Lyla but she clung on to him, dragging him backwards, and he managed to wrench free of her too late. Aleister was crouched beside Scarlett now, stroking her cheek with the very tip of the dagger. Even in an adult's body, Stanley wouldn't risk that knife piercing Scarlett's skin, and Aleister knew it. He gave a viscous laugh and Stanley was forced to watch his own lips cry out, 'Astaroth, hear us!'

'Astaroth, we command you!' Lyla joined, moving slowly towards her brother and Scarlett.

With a pang of despair, Stanley looked into Scarlett's terrified face. 'At least let me sit with her while you do it,' he said.

'With pleasure,' Lyla cackled. She turned to Aleister and together they began to chant, '*Anima Muto, Anima Muto...*'

The demon's throbbing glow shone brighter, Scarlett's face collapsing as Lyla grabbed her by the front of her t-shirt, kissing her full on lips. Scarlett made a squealing noise of protest but with her hands still tied there was little she could do to escape Lyla's vile embrace.

The lethal kiss continued and was sickening to watch. Stanley felt every drop of Aleister's foul blood drain into his feet as the seconds passed.

But now those seconds turned to a minute, and still they ticked on.

Lyla pushed Scarlett away from her and screamed. She turned furiously to the demon instead. 'Astaroth, I *command* you to obey me!'

Stanley could see the flames of hatred and fury blazing in the demon's flaming eyes. Its fury was unmistakable, and Stanley was alarmed to see how fast it was growing.

Lyla's own anger left no room for fear. Grabbing Scarlett again, she kissed her with even greater force, while Aleister stared defiantly at the demon, screaming '*Anima Muto*' at the top of his lungs.

Still nothing happened.

Stanley's hatred of the Cabells coursed through him like a tidal wave of boiling oil, but he fought to control it. The lodestone amulet must be protecting Scarlett, and the Cabells had no idea she was wearing it. This bought him some time. There was a chance to save Scarlett even if he could no longer save himself.

He glanced at Archibald, but the old man's eyes were fixed firmly on the raging demon; twisting and bulging, the fire of its skin spitting in all directions. When it suddenly turned its black eyes onto the old man he gave a tiny whimper and fell into a faint, his head lolling again. Millicent called his name, tapping his cheeks, but his flickering eyelids closed. It was clear that Stanley was on his own.

'Search her!' Lyla yelled. 'The spell worked last time. Something must be protecting her.'

The seconds ticked by like gunshots in Stanley's head. Whatever he was going to do, he must do it fast. He could wrestle the dagger from Aleister? No, it was two against one, and Scarlett might be hurt in the fight. What he needed was to use their own magic against them. Scanning the room for what felt like the hundredth time, Stanley's eyes landed on the glistening pile of spider web he had coughed up earlier. His heart gave a wild leap with an idea so completely perfect. His eyes moved to the cobwebs hanging all around the chapel.

'She's wearing an amulet,' Lyla shrieked. 'How could you not have checked for something like that, Aleister? She was locked up with the old fool long enough. He must've given it to her.'

'Well you didn't think of it either,' Aleister snarled back. Stanley could hear him grunting and Scarlett whimpering.

Aleister must be tugging at the string around her neck. But Stanley couldn't turn around. Not yet. Not before he'd found one. He scanned the dusty air. There were so many, but most were crumpled and lifeless, scrunched up like dead grass inside their broken webs.

Then he saw it, a movement by one of the candles. For a brief moment it had looked like a flickering flame, but how could it be when all the flames had risen up to form the demon? Stanley looked again. The spider was large, its jointed legs creeping over the candle, probably searching for somewhere to start a web.

There came a sickening yelp from Scarlett. Stanley turned to see Aleister ripping the amulet from her neck and throwing it across the room. The protection tablet lay abandoned on the floor beside him.

With not a single moment to waste, Stanley didn't dare check on the demon now as he leapt towards the spider, laying his hand before it and allowing it to climb onto his fingers. When he was sure he had it, he cupped his hands together, transferring the spider into one hand. Now, with his hand in a loose fist so as not to crush it, he shuddered when a few of its legs pushed through the gaps in his fingers.

Aleister turned. 'What are you doing?' he barked at Stanley. 'Get back over here where I can see you.'

Lyla crowed, 'Yes, you must watch the show, Stanley.' She turned her frosty blue stare onto Aleister. *Hurry up.* It's time to get this thing done once and for all.'

Aleister picked up the tablet again. There was horror in his eyes when he turned to face the demon. He couldn't seem to tear his gaze from its giant, bulging form, but with a deep, steadying breath the words of protection rang from his lips once more.

Stanley affected a wretched, broken expression as he dropped to his knees beside Scarlett.

'*Anima Muto!*' Lyla cried once more, her eyes dancing when she reached out to take Scarlett's face in her hands once more. She winked before pursing her thin lips and leaning in for the fatal kiss.

'Turn away, Scarlett,' Stanley whispered. '*Now.*'

Scarlett didn't need telling twice. With a frightened squeal, she swung her head to the side, just as Stanley pulled the spider from behind his back, pressing Lyla's forehead backwards with his free hand and letting the spider drop. The creature found its mark, landing on Lyla's lips, which had pulled back into a grimace of shock. When they opened suddenly into a long, furious scream, the scuttling spider disappeared into the black hole of Lyla's mouth.

Chapter Twenty-Six

To the Shores of the Lake of Fire

At the sound of Lyla's scream, Aleister stopped chanting, turning from the demon to discover his sister collapsed in a crumpled heap on the floor. 'What have you done, boy?' he thundered, racing to her side.

The spider had tumbled from her mouth and lay unnoticed beside her, its legs splayed in awkward directions, just like hers.

'I don't know what happened,' Stanley lied, praying that Aleister would not look up.

'*Lyla?*' Aleister dropped to his knees, grabbing her by the shoulders to shake her lifeless body. 'Wake up!' When she didn't move a pitiful wail escaped his trembling lips and he fell onto her chest, burying himself in her neck.

Silently, Stanley began to untie Scarlett.

'*Look,*' she whispered, pointing upwards. The two souls were circling each other, just like before, except this time one was tiny, its sparkling legs throwing out trails of ethereal light on its journey through the air. Then, like two comets crashing to earth, the souls flew into their new bodies.

Aleister must have felt something because he pulled his head up suddenly; Lyla's face opening its eyes and staring up at him. A moment later she was rolling around on her back, her limbs jerking at odd angles.

'What's wrong with you?' Aleister whimpered, turning white. He was watching his sister with a mixture of fear and disgust, having no idea that the spider's soul was now inside her body, stuck on its back. He jumped up, stumbling backwards away from her.

The spider meanwhile was scuttling around Aleister's feet. Stanley could just imagine Lyla's panic at finding herself in such a different body to the one she'd planned. She hopped over the floor more like a frog than a spider and Stanley guessed was desperately trying to get her brother's attention.

Aleister was unable to tear his eyes from Lyla's body, which had somehow got to its feet and was stumbling around the room, knocking over candles. Unused to a body with only two legs, the spider and was out of kilter, unable to balance itself in its effort to walk.

Scarlett let out another squeal. Lyla, inside the spider's body, had given a funny kind of jump, landing on Aleister's leg. A moment later she was climbing his jeans.

'Come on, now's our chance,' Stanley hissed. 'We'll grab Archie and Millicent and get out of here.'

But Scarlett didn't move; her face had contorted with a mixture of horror and fascination as she watched the spider. It had reached Aleister's chest, where its wiry legs clung desperately to Stanley's jumper.

When Aleister looked down and saw the spider, he let out a startled scream and swiped at it with the stone tablet, sending it flying across the room.

'He'll *kill* her if she comes back,' Scarlett said, her voice a quiver.

And it looked like she was right. Spider Lyla wasn't giving up. After a stunned moment of stillness, she was back up on her many legs, scurrying towards Aleister again in what must have been sheer panic.

'Aleister, don't!' Archibald screamed, waking up. 'It's *Lyl–*'

The name died on his lips. Aleister had brought his foot down on the spider, crushing it almost flat. It lay there twitching, Lyla's life ebbing visibly away.

Archibald began to sob. 'You poor, *stupid…*' His words drowned among flowing tears.

Aleister looked from the dying spider to his sister's stumbling body and the terrible realisation distorted his face. He fell to his knees again, this time the tablet tumbling from his hand, landing with the sound of cracking stone.

'Hold the tablet together again, Aleister. Recite the words!' Archibald's plea was loud and desperate. But Aleister was deaf to his uncle's screams. Scooping the spider up, he rocked back and forth, staring down into his open hands, his face twisted like a torn painting. He began to cry, his chest rising and falling jaggedly as his sobs built to a miserable choir.

The sound tore into Stanley's hatred of the Cabells, ripping it apart. He could read the grief in Aleister's eyes like a tragic novel. Aleister had lived his entire life with Lyla, built everything around her; saw his future forever entwined with hers. Now it was over and in this moment, however despicable their plans had been, Stanley couldn't help seeing the Cabells as victims of their own unhappiness and greed.

Yet compassion did not stay long in Stanley's chest. It was chased out by a deafening roar that rung through the chapel. Soon they were engulfed in a heat so mighty, it threatened to melt the skin from their bodies.

'Ashtoreth's coming!' Archibald shrieked.

Stanley leapt across the room towards the discarded lodestone amulet, sweat flying from his skin as he flung the amulet around Scarlett's neck, before pulling her close.

'How *dare* you defy us, Astaroth!' Aleister spat suddenly. He was on his feet, his expression devastated and furious in equal measure. He screamed at the terrible, pulsing form of the demon with a flashing stare that was no longer afraid. 'We conjured you; *we* are your masters! Bring my sister back!'

The demon only grew bigger, burning ever hotter. When it threw back its horned head and laughed, the terrible sound sliced through Stanley's soul like a jagged knife. He looked to Archibald, who answered the question before he could ask it.

'With the protection tablet broken the demon is breaking free,' he shrieked, pointing to the sea of fire the demon was growing out of. 'You have to put the fire out, Stanley. Use the altar cloth!'

At these words the writhing demon turned its gaze onto Stanley, the black pits of its eyes stretching to the size of two caves.

A frightened snake coiled inside Stanley's stomach, but somehow he pushed himself past the demon to reach the altar, grabbing the cloth that covered it. When he turned again to face the flaming beast it was so hot he felt as though he were standing on the edge of a volcano. Worse than that, the creature had grown so enormous the altar cloth looked like a handkerchief against its sheer size. With a desperate cry Stanley threw the cloth against the demonic flames.

Just as he'd feared, it burned away in seconds. They were too late and, this time, it was Millicent's turn to faint. Dragging Scarlett towards her and Archibald, Stanley could only watch the cloth's charred remains being sucked into the smouldering flames.

Then came the explosion. A blast so powerful they were blinded by searing light and heat. Stanley heard the splinter of wood and glass as the tiny windows shattered and the chapel door burst out of its frame, landing somewhere among the trees outside.

He wasn't sure how much time had passed when he woke up face down on the floor again. Sweltering heat surged into his skin, while a biting mixture of smoke and the stench of something vile and putrid gnawed at his nose and throat.

'*Stanley..?*

He stretched out a hand to Scarlett, who was coughing beside him.

'What – is – *that?*' she said in a strangled whisper.

Stanley pulled himself onto his back, a creeping dread

gluing his eyes shut. He could hear a loud wind whistling through the room, and it was growing stronger, hot air lapping at his skin each time it passed.

Forcing his eyes open, Stanley's breath caught sharply in his throat. A mass of blood red smoke was circling the chapel. It was pulsing and twisting; all the while moving closer and closer to Aleister, who was staring up at it, his eyes stretched in horror.

Aleister. Stanley could hardly believe it; Aleister's body was standing over there. So that must mean... Stanley glanced down to see his own legs, inside his own jeans. He pulled his hands in front of his face. The fingers that moved were small and clean of blood and... *his.* He laughed out loud.

Scarlett turned to face him. 'Stanley, you're *you,* I– I don't believe it.'

They both looked to Archibald, who was staring back at them, relief competing with the terror on his face. 'Astaroth has reversed the spell,' he breathed, his eyes darting after the red smoke, 'The demon was forced to perform the *Anima Muto* spell under enslavement and would never honour it now that its...' Archibald's voice began to shake. 'Now that its... br–broken *free.*'

Archibald gathered Millicent gently up in his arms, beckoning to Stanley and Scarlett, who made their way towards him, clinging to each other all the while. They stood in a huddle, immobile with terrified fascination, watching the progress of the terrible red smoke.

What had began as a formless red mass was taking shape. Thick smoky tendrils grew into arms that wrapped around Aleister. A pair of horns appeared and Aleister let out a terrible cry. It soon became heart-stoppingly clear that the demon's shape was forming around him, swallowing him whole. Aleister's clawing hands shot out from inside the thick cloud of smoke. Hands that clutched at thin air in a bid to escape, and then vanished again. Soon he was completely lost to sight inside the whirling smoke.

The smoke began to thin; it seemed to be slowly dissolving. It was soon clear that something else entirely was happening. They could hear Aleister's moans and yelps and a moment later his body was revealed, the smoke seeping into every inch of him, until, with a final gasp, he had absorbed the last red wisp into his shaking body.

Aleister fell silent and a look of calm self-assurance came over his face. He gave a long blink and Scarlett screamed. Instead of human eyes, Aleister's face held two pools of vivid crimson. Specks of dancing fire burst from where pupils should have been, those flames soon spreading to the rest of his eyes.

Aleister's lips parted into a gruesome smile and when he spoke his voice took on a low snake-like hiss. 'Aleister and Lyla Cabell,' the voice said, 'such deluders. Not once did they offer me an oath loyal with meaning.' He began to move slowly around the room, those livid eyes dancing over the piles of debris that made up the chapel. 'Nothing but a pair of inept conjurers with the impertinence to enslave and command one such as myself.' Here he turned to focus those two fiery holes on his stupefied audience, '*Astaroth,* the greatest Fire Lord that ever was. The Grand Duke of the Hidden Realms.' A pitiless smile curled his lips. 'Now I will take my revenge.'

'Please,' Archibald gasped, passing Millicent shakily to

Stanley and stepping forward. 'Lord Astaroth, take your revenge on me. The fault in all this is mine alone.'

Despite its flaming eyes, the demon's laugh was a cold, hollow echo. 'The only souls I require today belong to the Cabells, twisted and burned by selfishness and greed.' A tongue of glistening skin, like a lizard's, licked Aleister's lips greedily. '*Hers* I have, and *his* will follow shortly. They will join my family then at the Lake of Fire, where they will truly discover the extent of the Grand Duke's powers.' Astaroth fixed Stanley and Scarlett with that fiery stare. 'You children have a lifetime to curse your souls, and when you do, I'll be ready to collect.'

Stanley was speaking before he could stop himself. 'Wh– what do you mean?' he spluttered. 'How will we curse our souls?'

'In your heart, your bones, you *know*, boy,' the demon replied. The abandoned Book flew now into Aleister's outstretched hand. 'The greatest power within these pages will always reside within the Dark. Aleister Cabell was right about one thing; *this* old man has been too weak to use it properly.' Astaroth spat these last words at Archibald, causing burning sparks to fly from Aleister's lips. 'You children will be different; you will both succumb to temptation, just as the Cabells did before you. I am certain of it. Your souls are already mine.'

Scarlett's fingers locked into Stanley's. He could feel their combined strength growing as together they held the imperious gaze of this ancient malign force. Almost at the same time, they said, 'You're wrong.'

The demon laughed its mirthless laugh again, and they all

watched in horror as Aleister's skin began to glow ruby red. For a moment his eyes flashed back to human, and held a wretched, piercing fear. Then, with an ear-splitting scream, he was propelled into the air, where he hovered long enough for them all to shrink backwards to the chapel's edge, before he exploded into flames.

Withered specks of ash floated down to lay silently on the cold stones, where Aleister had stood only moments ago; a few final tendrils of ruby smoke vanishing through the floor.

In the stunned silence that followed, Stanley noticed a tiny movement where the spider lay. Its splayed legs twitched and it began to wriggle. Scarlett followed where Stanley was looking and seemed to muster herself. She walked slowly over to the spider, bending down and gently gathering the tiny creature up in her hands. Meeting Stanley's startled gaze with a smile, she turning it right way up without flinching, before placing it carefully down on the floor again. They watched the spider scuttle away, back to the darkness and safety of the quiet chapel.

'The poor thing never hurt anyone,' Scarlett said.

A laugh tickled Stanley's throat, but quickly vanished again. Something else had caught his eye. It was Lyla's body lying on the floor, silent and still, her eyes open, staring into nothing. Scarlett had seen it too and she ran suddenly to stand back beside Archibald.

'Don't be afraid,' Stanley heard the old man whisper. He took Scarlett's hand, walking with her to where Lyla lay. Gazing down at Lyla, he said, 'She died moments after Astaroth returned her to her own body. I watched her breathe her last.'

Stanley moved to join them and there was real sadness in Archibald's eyes when he looked back up at the children. 'Her soul was then the demon's to claim.'

'And Astaroth took Aleister too?' Stanley asked, although he wasn't sure he wanted to hear the answer.

Archibald gave a resigned nod. 'A Fire Lord is made entirely of burning, negative energy,' he said. 'Aleister's body could only contain it for so long.' He sighed. 'My niece and nephew sealed their fate the moment they ventured into the Darkness. The spell may have cursed their bodies, but they alone cursed their souls, twisted them into something fit only for the Lake of Fire.'

'Will the demon be back?' Scarlett asked, trembling.

'No,' Archibald replied. He gave a weary smile. 'Unless either of you wish to summon it?'

Stanley's eyes wandered over the destroyed chapel, the fallen body of Lyla and the pile of still smouldering ash that was once Aleister, eventually returning Archibald's steady gaze. 'Only when that Lake of Fire freezes over.'

Scarlett gave a nervous laugh and took Stanley's hand, as Archibald reached out to take Millicent again. He whispered softly in her ear until, slowly, she woke up. Travelling around the chapel, her glistening eyes stretched wide in disbelief. 'Is it over?' she breathed.

'Yes, it's over,' Archibald replied, smiling. 'And don't worry, my dearest friend, we'll have you fit and well again before you can say *Restorative Remember*. And as soon as we're both back to full health our adventures will begin.'

A smile lit Millicent's face and Scarlett reached out a tentative hand to stroke her gently behind the ears. 'I'm so sorry I thought badly of you before, Millicent,' she said.

'No sorries needed,' Millicent replied. Her voice was weak but full of its usual kindness. She turned suddenly back to Archie. 'What do you mean, *adventures?*'

'My ingredients stores are somewhat low,' he said, an eyebrow flickering. 'They need replenishing.' For a moment something like shame crumpled his face. 'I'm afraid I let my niece and nephew change me, even before that blighted Befuddlement Brew. I've hidden myself away for too long; stopped exploring, *collecting*, like I used to.' He smiled. 'If what happened here has taught me anything, it's that life is short and precious, you can't let fear destroy who you are, your hopes and dreams.' He beamed now at Stanley and Scarlett. 'You have shown true spirit and bravery, children; don't ever stop being who you are. Seize every opportunity life offers you, or before you know it, you'll look in the mirror and realise that you're almost one hundred years old.' He winked. 'Not that you should let that stop you.'

Raising Millicent higher in his arms, Archibald Marble exclaimed, 'It's time to go back out into the world, my dear, to move among the communities of hidden species, flora a*nd* fauna; whatever and wherever they may be. We'll seek them out together and learn everything we can from them.'

'And will you teach u*s?*' Stanley said suddenly. 'Scarlett and me.'

'In time,' Archibald replied, his eyes dancing now with some secret fire. 'I'll teach you everything I know.'

For a long moment they stood wordlessly together. Then, as one, they turned their backs on the chapel, and stepped out into the warm dark night.

One
Year Later

the
Crackshaw
family
Marble Manor

Marble Manor

FROG
BURPS

'Look, Stanley, another postcard!' Scarlett stumbled out of the fireplace, her face a blaze of excitement. She waved the picture of a tropical jungle at him. 'You'll never believe where they are now.'

Stanley glanced up, a tiny glass bottle hovering in his hand. He was mid-way through brewing an arthritis remedy and had one more important ingredient to add. 'Wait just one sec,' he said, his tongue poking out in concentration. 'If I don't add the exact amount of cobra venom we could end up with some stingy side-effects.'

There was a bellow of laughter from an armchair by the fire. 'We certainly don't want a repeat of last week,' Dad exclaimed, closing the book he'd been reading with a dusty thud. 'Your mum turning poor Aunt Ada's bonce blue with that tonsillitis tonic.'

Mum gave a small cough from her place at the workbench. 'I just used the wrong type of beetle, that's all. Ada's throat got better, didn't it? So there was no *real* harm done.'

Scarlett giggled. 'Still don't think she'll be coming to visit us again any time soon.'

'There,' said Stanley, with a satisfied grin. The yellow liquid in his bowl was now bubbling gently. 'Perfect.' He turned to Scarlett. 'So what are they up to now?'

She handed him the postcard, gabbling before he had the chance to read it. 'They're in Borneo. Can you believe Archie made it to the top of Mount Kinabalu? And they've been canoeing down the Kapuas; remember he told us it was his lifelong dream? Millicent got cuttings from a *cat's whiskers* plant. Archie says the leaves can be used to treat –'

'– The bladder and kidneys?' Stanley asked quickly.

'Correct!' Scarlett replied, beaming.

Dad moved to stand between his two children. 'With brains like these it won't be long till the *Crankshaw Family Apothecary* is open for business,' he said, laying an arm over each of their shoulders.

'And your book will be published soon,' Mum said. '*The Secret History of Marble Manor.* We're all so proud of you, Will.'

'I still can't believe old man Marble gave us this house.' Dad gazed around the room, blinking back tears. 'To live and work within its wondrous walls, could life get any better?'

'Oh no, he's off again,' Stanley grinned. 'You really should try and toughen up a bit, Dad.'

'Yeah, yeah, I get it,' laughed Dad. 'All that time we thought you were being, well... *over-sensitive*, but you were right all along. About everything.'

Mum's frown reached every part of her face. 'When I think what could've happened to you and your sister without your intuition, Stanley,' she said with a shudder. 'It just doesn't bear thinking about.'

'What was it Archie called you again?' Scarlett asked.

'An *empath*,' Stanley replied. 'Apparently it means I'm more tuned in to other people's energies and emotions, so I can sense things, you know, that other people can't.' He shrugged, although his heart was secretly swelling with pride. 'He could be right, I s'pose.'

Scarlett's voice broke the thoughtful silence that followed. 'Um, do you ever *feel* the Cabells, you know, around the Manor?'

Stanley's mind wandered through the section of forest

where they'd scattered Aleister's ashes, to Lyla's grave near the chapel. The only thing that touched his senses was a distant memory. He shook his head. 'No. They've gone. For good.'

'Poor Archie,' Scarlett said now. 'He still thinks it was all his fault.'

Mum sighed. 'Just like the Book of Wonders, Aleister and Lyla had a darkness inside them, it's true. But we all dream in light and shade; all manner of voices murmur at our hearts.' She smiled at Stanley and Scarlett in turn. 'It's the ones we listen to that make us who we are; our choices that define us. Always remember: your lives belong to you and no one else.'

Dad twitched an eyebrow. 'Very wise, Nelly my dear, Archibald would be proud of how much you've learned from him.'

Mum gave Dad a little shove. 'Yes, he would,' she chuckled, before turning to Scarlett. 'Did Archie say if he's used that Confuddlement Charm on the palm oil growers yet? It's a disgrace what those plantations are doing to the natural forests. There won't be any orangutans left if they carry on.'

'Soon,' Scarlett nodded, grinning. 'He's got it all planned out, like always.'

Stanley followed her gaze to a locked iron cabinet that sat in the very centre of the room, and a shiver of pleasure passed through him. This was where they'd all agreed to keep the Book of Wonders while Archie and Millicent were away. Stanley's eyes wandered to the strange-smelling packages that had been delivered to Marble Manor ever since the adventuring duo had arrived in Asia, all carrying strict instructions not to be opened until their return.

'Only a week to go,' he said, voice trembling slightly. 'Then our lessons *really* begin.'

They were going to open the Book of Wonders. To journey together through the whispered secrets of its pages. Stanley was going to be a magician, a true and adept mage.

Life would never be neat and normal again.

MILLICENT
the
MAGNIFICENT

Elizabeth Waight

Elizabeth is a Londoner who loves exploring and has lived in many different countries around the world. Her jobs have ranged from door-to-door saleswoman to shark chaser, but her passion has always been for telling stories. She's never fitted into a neat normal box (hoorah)— in fact her friends suspect she's a witch. She hopes they are right. She currently lives in East London with her grumpy cat Ziggy and dreams of living by the sea.

Jenny Law

Jenny grew up on the inner-city council estates of 1980s London. She could always be found sat outside her block of flats drawing in her sketchbook; come rain or shine she'd be surrounded by the neighbourhood cats. Her colourful bohemian younger years inspire her playful and somewhat mischievous illustrations. Jenny lives in London with her two children, husband, two sassy cats and Dolly Bubbles the chihuahua. She works as both an illustrator and a designer.

Lightning Source UK Ltd.
Milton Keynes UK
UKHW012343071220
374785UK00003B/791